For the woman who gave me life.

I Love You, Mom

THE GHOST
OF
CHRISTMAS PAST

A NOVELLA

MICHAEL HEBLER

ᛕ

Library of Congress Control Number: 2016908959
BIASC Category: Literary Fiction

ISBN: 978-0-6926740-8-6
eBook ISBN: 978-0-9833884-8-7

Book design by Michael Hebler
Author portrait by Manuela Ruggeri

Manufactured in the United States of America

10 9 8 7 6 5 4 3 2 1

CONTENTS

THE GHOST
OF
CHRISTMAS PAST

STAVE ONE

Sara and the Spirit

An unnatural presence was near; that was certain. Sara Bello felt its proximity once snapping out of her daydream; though to call it a daydream when occurring in the middle of the night could be considered irresponsible or misleading. I have no such intention of either, I only mean that the hour of the day is far too important to be distorted. I will now put an end to this clause.

Sara awoke, and that was that, having been trapped in a careless daze since leaving her apartment in the early hour. She did not feel the abnormal presence at the start of her meandering; she perceived it only once she had stepped onto a residential street that was shrouded in darkness.

Though you and I know better, because we are aware of the topic of this grand adventure, Sara blamed her uneasiness on her environment. Any number of things, or a combination thereof, could affect the senses: the frigid air that nipped at her mind as well as her nose, the loneliness of the day even while waiting for a stop light on a crowded corner, or the neglected and precarious neighborhood in which Sara found herself wandering. Though caught unaware, she was not startled, for her heavy thoughts had been just as morose as her surroundings.

Sara shut her eyes, and then opened them much slower than they had closed. Nothing had changed. The street continued to repel light, as though itself was a living thing that was frightened or susceptible to illumination. Street lamp bulbs were burnt out, home windows were dark, even the black and gray clouds

3

layering the atmosphere doused any radiance from the moon and stars; thereby creating a dull and ominous glow which allowed Sara to see no more than twenty feet in whichever direction. For any next woman, or man, one would turn back the way they come and retreat quietly, hoping that whomever, or whatever, that may be lurking wouldn't follow; but not Sara. In fact, she welcomed the disquieting sensation, as though opening a door for any such stranger and inviting him out of the cold and into the warmth of her hopelessness.

On only one other occasion during her journey, which had begun hours ago while walking out the front door of her eight-hundred square foot, two-thousand dollar a month, rodent-inhabited apartment, did Sara remember being mindful of her surroundings. The department store display of holiday cheer on Manhattan's 34th Street could knock the sight back into any blind man... well, not physically, of course, but the luster had been apropos for this Christmas Eve; extravagant and joyful with mannequins dressed in expensive luxury while standing in glistening fake white snow next to a wall of well-synchronized television programming.

However, when Sara stopped to take notice, it had not been to ooh and ahh at the exhibit intended to coerce the rich to buy more and to make the poor feel less fortunate. Instead, she glared back at her reflection; the remorseful and sullen woman who had not been part of the original envisioning for this display (for no reasonable or sane designer would want to include the life-worn face of a forty-three-year-old woman with dried tears crusted on her cheeks). Just as well, the snowflakes that gathered on her brow and eyelashes turned her stringy black and gray hair white, as well as her native Cuban cocoa complexion into a ghostly sight. Each passerby who dared to notice Sara glaring at the window, looking like a mannequin herself, did not see such a melancholy woman, but only a late shopper intrigued by the broadcast of a Christmas parade on the multitude of screens.

The final shot of Santa waving to hundreds of admiring spectators switched to two newscasters behind a station desk. On the screen below flashed the closed caption words, "God bless Us, Every One," next to a digital clock counting down the final seconds to Christmas. Sara had withdrawn at that moment. She turned and walked as aimlessly as a dead leaf fluttering in an autumn wind while the nearby Catholic Churches uniformly rang their bells. The welcoming of the first hour of the new day had been announced. December twenty-fifth had arrived.

Sara's feet dragged. Without the gleam of light to distract the desolate neighborhood street, the sound of her mud-caked soles scraping against the concrete amplified. She continued onward, daring and unafraid. Even the homeless man, or possibly woman, at the top of a brownstone's stoop, who stirred restlessly beneath a pile of newspapers, gave her not the slightest pause. She feared nothing, or so she thought until frigid anxiety froze her where she stood; and not the cold. Sara scrubbed away the ice with her feet, uncovering two child-sized hand imprints in the concrete showing the name Sara beneath one and Danny below the other. She gazed at the haunting impressions that somehow could be seen in the dark. Sara knew precisely what neighborhood she had ambled into and on which street she stood.

She spat a few unpleasant words for her subconscious bringing her here. Then, as though being pulled by a human magnet, she twisted towards the homeless mound and glowered at the front door behind which it slept. Sara turned her gaze to the sky, her vision reaching all the way up to the third story before a layer of gloom concealed what rose beyond.

The structure towered above her like the phantom of a menacing giant, although a sleeping giant, for it was dark between the cracks of the lumber barricade that crisscrossed the front door, as well as each shattered window. However, a single window's glass on the third level was the exception. Somehow it had remained intact and unobstructed, appearing as though the giant possessed one good eye.

She glared at the pane with sinful spite when, as mysteriously as the lost city of Atlantis or the Voynich Manuscript, the giant's eye opened to wink at her.

Disgust consumed Sara. She thought, *What reason did it have to do that? Was it provoking me? Mocking me?* If she had something to blind it with, then it would be done.

And like a Christmas miracle, Sara's silent prayer was answered when she stepped on a rock while backing away from the brownstone. Picking up the stone, she cocked her arm and posed in a pitching stance to make good on her intentions when...

"Hey! Don't do that!" The demanding voice seemingly came from nowhere--like a ghost.

She turned on the spot but continued to keep her grip firm on the stone; ready to launch at her new target, if need be. But the cab driver poking his head out the passenger window did not appear to be any threat. Her grip relaxed.

"Maybe you shouldn't be out here alone?" he advised.

"I can handle myself."

"I only mean because it's Christmas. Don't you got somewhere better to be?"

Sara stayed silent, as though not knowing how to respond.

"I could give you a lift if you ain't goin' far. No charge."

"See if he needs a lift instead."

"Who?"

Sara turned. She had every intention of pointing to the one who had articles, stock prices, theatre times, and classifieds keeping him warm, but he…she…it was gone--vanished--as though never there.

Flabbergasted! (In its strongest sense of the word) Sara gaped at the space on the stoop, befuddled and aghast. Then, not knowing how to explain her testimony to the man, or perhaps fearing that the cab and its driver would be figments too, she dropped the rock and walked on.

Sara kept her pace steady; as one would when denying that they had ever stopped walking. She pressed on, ignoring the driver's pleas in much the same way as she ignored the fire hydrant, or the trash can, or the burnt lamppost she passed. Instead, her concentration focused on where to go next and what to do once she arrived.

"Come on. It's cold. It's Christmas. Let me do a good deed. I kinda need to, you know?"

No, Sara thought, *I do not 'know.'*

"Look! Anywhere you want. It ain't even gotta be that

close."

She stopped walking and turned. Based on his annoying persistence, Sara had come to believe that this man, unlike the other from the stoop, was not her imagination's creation.

The driver exited his side quickly to come around and open the back door.

"Anywhere I want?" she confirmed first.

"Sure! I mean, within reason. I can't take ya to California or Florida."

Sara climbed into the back seat, behind the steel mesh that separated her from the driver's domain. The man closed the door before dropping back behind the steering wheel that protruded from the dash next to a taxi meter which gave the time: 12:41.

"Where to?"

She did not know yet. "Just drive."

#

Five minutes into the ride, the driver, whose name remained a mystery to Sara, had asked "You know where yet?" three more times. And at each bequest, Sara did not answer. Instead, she fixed her gaze on the city through the mud-splattered window, which made for a bleak and dismal view. But the filthy glass did not influence Sara's view of the world; she perceived it as such at all times.

Sara couldn't look his way even if she had wanted to. Aware that he was keeping a close eye on her through the rearview, it was his kind eyes that she could not bear looking into. Not that

8

she found him attractive by any means (thoughts of romance had no business being in the company of despair), but with leather-toned skin similar to her own and dark brown eyes that matched the color of his well-kept short hair and van dyke, he was pleasant looking enough. In fact, if Sara were in a guessing mood, she would have thought the driver to be near her age, only the years hadn't reflected as harshly on him.

Upon his fourth request, Sara responded abruptly with "Keep going north," hoping to appease the driver for a handful of minutes.

But the man refused her a moments' peace. "You visit your family yet?"

Sara hesitated; and had he allowed her time to reply with either a "No" or a "Yes," she would have. But therein resided her continued hesitation. Both were a lie, and her decision had been stuck on the moral of whether to tell the courteous driver the smaller, or the larger, of her two lies. As it were, Sara had no family, and the latter would not only "confirm" that she had someone to visit, but that she had done so while the former merely "implied" that she had a family still to visit. In actuality, Sara thought neither were any of this man's business, but he had been much too eager for a conversation to wait for her nonsense.

"I haven't. It's not that I don't want to, but with work and everything…"

"Life's rough." End of conversation, if Sara had any say.

She turned to the window in hopes of returning to solace, but the driver continued watching her through the caged partition, as though he were a child on his first visit to the zoo.

9

It was her own fault; Sara was sure. Had she made an attempt to disguise her downcast disposition, even a little, perhaps he would have let her be. But, oh, the effort to camouflage the tiniest speck of her hardship would take more strength than what she was willing to give this life. Still, she could not bear being continuously ogled.

"You got a problem...?" then fixated on the license to retrieve the driver's name, but instead, Sara had her attention drawn to the picture of a young silver-haired boy, who could have been no more than fifteen. She blinked multiple times then rubbed her eyes before focusing on the picture that then mirrored the driver's image.

"Sorry," he defended. "It's just... you seem familiar to me... like we've met before."

"I don't believe this." Sara rolled her eyes into the back of her head.

"Hey, don't get the wrong idea, lady, I didn't mean anything by it."

The adamant driver continued to babble about her misunderstanding. Sara tried to ignore the man, but he insisted on being heard, going on and on about the confusion. And she had very nearly reached her limit, ready to bark something unkind, when Sara looked past the driver and caught a glimpse of the George Washington Bridge between the moving skyscrapers.

There was no hesitation in her voice when she interrupted with the order to "Take the GW."

The driver waved a finger to indicate that he had heard her without a single hiccup in his spiel, "I'm serious! It ain't a line.

I'm married! Got a baby girl too... Sara."

He then fished out his wallet to dig for a picture. The driver dropped a small photo into the cash tray beneath the wired mesh. Sara retrieved the image of the happiest girl she ever did see, posing on Santa Claus's lap.

"Fifteen months. She's a real cutie, ain't she? Takes after me!"

Sara smiled without meaning to. She wanted to ask, *Why the name Sara? What significance was it to him?* Her experience with the name had brought nothing but misery and solitude.

And for that reason, she retreated from her inquiry and threw the photo back into the tray as though it were a venomous snake ready to strike. She then followed her volatility by repeating the order, "I said, the GW," with firmer conviction then previously.

"Yeah. I heard ya."

She caught a glimpse of the man's disappointed eyes falling from the mirror to the road before she too, returned hers to the soiled window.

The driver had steered them along the Hudson River. No lights, no Christmas cheer. The view of the dismal surrounding shoreline reclaimed Sara's dark mood, finding some warmth in its cold comfort.

#

12:54

Sara would not have noticed the time on the fare calculator if she hadn't looked towards the driver when he asked, "So, what'd that building ever do to you? Why were you gonna throw that rock?" She would have answered the man if her current despair hadn't refused to release her attention. She returned her gaze to the window, and focused on how she would convince the driver to pull over to the side and let her out of his cab once halfway across the bridge.

Sara had no desire for this life. She could no longer blame the universe, and everything under its shroud, for her misery but only herself for allowing her to become its victim. To her, that point had been reached, but the curious thing was that she never uttered a word to the driver; not out loud, at least. So, how he knew what she was pondering remained a mystery... for now.

"Suicide's always up on Christmas Eve. I get that life ain't perfect; far from it, I know, but to end this amazing chance you've been given just don't make no sense to me."

"What do you mean, *'you know'*?" Sara challenged.

But given no time to reply, the driver slowed at the first sight of red and blue emergency lights dancing over the steel scaffold. "Aw, Christ. There's been an accident."

Let it be known that the driver should not be blamed for what happened next. The accident's disruption had been so hypnotizing that he did not notice the open door and empty back seat until it was too late.

He hollered, "Hey, wait," which Sara heard faintly in the distance, but ignored, as she raced along the bridge's walkway.

Once the overlying commotion of the unfortunate accident dulled to a low hum, Sara stopped running.

She paused before a second railing as though it were a

gate waiting to be opened. This setback would be her final hurdle, and once traversed… freedom.

Sara cast a glance in all directions to be sure she was alone, but one other presence was nearby; however, he, she, or it, was welcomed. Though invisible, Sara perceived Death standing by her side, and felt the touch of compassion. There was some relief to know that Death was not too busy with the passengers of the accident. She did not wish harm on anyone, other than herself; *unless*, she thought, *Death had already taken care of that business.* In any case, Sara was happy to believe that the invisible specter now stood by her side.

Sara climbed over the second rail. Her breathing did not hasten, nor did she experience even the slightest twinge of fear. Her movement felt as natural as breathing. She peered downward to where the river flowed but only saw a dark void; endless, yet inviting. Knowing that she would not be able to see the water until she was upon it made her decision to keep her eyes shut the whole way down an easy one. Any pain would be swift before absolute numbness set in.

The sound of church bells from the New Jersey shore approached from the left as identical bells from the right chimed in from Manhattan. They announced the one o'clock hour in the same moment Sara let go of the railing.

Her arms spread out like lifeless branches. The cold wind intensified as it blew past her body, which had an odd warmth within it. Sara felt free and happy; it was everything she had hoped. Of all the choices she made in life, *This one was good.*

The air surrounding her no longer felt cold. Sara assumed

that the end of her life had come.

But where was the impact? Where was the hard smack of the icy river?

It could be presumed that the freezing wind during her descent had numbed her body so thoroughly that she felt nothing, but then, that would contradict the warmth she felt currently.

Deciding to look for herself, Sara opened her eyes and was greeted by her reflection consumed in an aura of flames. The most viable and fitting explanation would be that Sara had passed beyond this world and entered the realm where fire, and its counterpart, brimstone, thrived well. It's been said that is where tortured souls go when leaving the earth unnaturally. However, her reflection was not as pristine as though looking in a mirror, but warped and rippled like on a water's surface.

I haven't hit yet?! Her mind screamed.

Not a moment later, did Sara realize that she was not moving towards the water but, in fact, across it. Even more astounding was the fact that a young hand held hers.

She turned to gaze at a figure, not a man or woman but more like a boy or girl, who held Sara up without venture. Surely the girl, or boy, or whatever the being, was unlike any image of Death Sara had considered. Its appearance was gentle and pleasant with long aged hair that did not flap in the soaring wind but lay across its equally white tunic instead. But the odd thing of it was--should the preceding not be considered odd at all--the sprig of holly carried in the hand that touched hers and a nightcap the thing held in the other.

The figure's head turned. It smiled at her when advising,

THE GHOST OF CHRISTMAS PAST

"Do not release me."

#

Sara did not need to speak a single word. The Spirit knew much with just a touch of her hand; things even she was not aware of about herself. It understood every moment of her past from an aspiration to be an attorney of law to her failure to become one, though her most notable regret was the brother she had allowed to be taken away from her when they were just children.

The details of Sara's past were as clear to the Spirit as her face when it looked towards her puzzled expression while ascending above the city. She was not frightened but bewildered by her current situation, contemplating whether she was dead, dreaming, or insane. And the Spirit knew which she prayed to be true. It knew all it needed to begin her journey of retrospect and rekindling—as the Spirit had done with so many souls before hers. But first, they needed to reach their destination, which had just come into view.

Sara's grip tightened. Her confusion had transitioned into anxiety by seeing the familiar front door. They approached the brownstone swiftly then soared through the door as though it were made of air. Then the Spirit, being a human-like candle in appearance, illuminated the darkened hallway with its radiant glow.

Only once it was safe to do so, Sara pulled her hand away upon landing, but not before the Spirit perceived her intention to curse it for bringing her back to this abandoned beast. However, Sara said nothing, but instead gawked at each part of herself that

15

she could view. Her legs, feet, hands, fingers… all were solid and still covered with flesh.

"I ain't dead?" she asked, disappointedly.

"No," replied the Spirit, in a soft voice that echoed as though coming from across a large empty room, and yet its countenance was clearly at Sara's side.

"Who are you?"

"I am what was; the visions from days long forgotten, and the spirit of humanity during the season of joy. I am the Spirit of Christmas' Past."

Sara gaped at the Spirit for a moment.

"Spirit, huh? Are you a boy spirit, or girl spirit? I can't tell."

"Gender has no bearing in the afterlife."

"I thought you said I wasn't dead?"

"It is only *I* who am a spirit."

"You saved my life then?" She challenged, as noted by the inflection of resentment in her inquiry.

"It was not your time."

"What makes you think you know when it's my time?"

"Time is what I know."

Sara paused, as though struggling to make sense of her situation. Failure to find it ended her silence. "Christmas past, right? My past?"

It nodded.

"Did we just fly through a door?"

It mimicked its previous nod.

THE GHOST OF CHRISTMAS PAST

Sara touched the Spirit's flame. Her reach was slow and hypnotic. The Spirit could sense her pleasure with the treasures its fire offered.

"It ain't hot."

"The light I bestow reveals the memories kept in shadow. To keep your reflections in darkness, you need but to thrust this cap upon my head and extinguish me."

Sara's eyes flipped to the nightcap. The Spirit listened to her mind consider putting an end to this interruption. It slipped the nightcap out of her reach.

She peered at the Spirit's young face and the eyes that revealed its endless age and wisdom. Then, turning to her surroundings, Sara saw that the Spirit's light had been replaced by light coming from the hallway's fixtures, having returned to their purpose. The long forgotten grimy and battered corridor had been refreshed. A coat of lacquer glistened on its wood-paneled frame, accompanied by the pleasant sounds of Bing Crosby's White Christmas from the next room, and the aroma of turkey, pumpkin, and a hodgepodge of spices that seeped in from a kitchen. Sara recognized the time as being thirty-eight years ago… to the very night.

"This was your home."

"It was my prison," she corrected instantly.

"These walls hold the memories of a past, which you have long forgotten."

"Forgotten?!" She roared. "I didn't forget nothing."

Sara caught her breath then jumped out of the path of a young girl who darted from the parlor to the kitchen. The five-year-old was no stranger to Sara. She was Lydia Clark; at least, that was her surname before being adopted.

"They cannot see us. These are but reflections of a past, which cannot be altered."

Then, with only the warning of thundering footsteps, a troop of seven more children, raced, giggling as they ran.

A knock came from the front door. Like the call of the school bell for the children, a woman, much like a spirit herself, pivoted from the corner.

Sara froze like ice. Miss Darnell, the thin woman with graying hair wound tightly into a bun was a horrific sight.

"There is to be no running!" She ordered.

Sara shivered.

Instinctively, she stepped sideways to avoid the marching woman as her low heels clocked towards the door.

Outside, a rookie police officer held a two-year-old boy in his arms. At his side stood a woman in her twenties, holding onto the hand of a frightened little girl. Sara recognized her five-year-old self instantly, as well as her baby brother, Danny.

Miss Darnell stepped to the side--a less than enthusiastic invitation for the pair to enter with the children.

"Good evening. Are you Agatha Darnell?" The chipper lady asked before stepping inside.

"I am," Miss Darnell confirmed coldly, the perfect opposition to the other's sunny disposition.

"I'm Amy Valentine from Child Protective Services. We spoke on the phone."

"I know," she affirmed while glaring at the two children.

"And this is Sara and Daniel Bello."

"Danny," corrected young Sara.

Miss Darnell's intense attention focused on the little girl. "His name is Daniel, and that is what I will call him, and so will you while in my house."

The glare between young Sara and Miss Darnell could not be cut through with a saw if tried. The stares put a halt to any further discussion or movement.

While not as much as a breath was inhaled, Sara considered that perhaps the Spirit had halted this memory, but within seconds, Miss Darnell broke the silence by addressing Amy Valentine sternly, "I cannot guarantee they will be kept together. Most new parents cannot accommodate two children, and two-year-old boys are in higher demand than five-year-old girls."

Sara recalled those venomous words as though they had been uttered to her in the last hour. Their harshness put Amy into a near catatonic state.

The rookie cop came to their defense. "You always talk like that in front of kids?"

"Officer, these children are orphans now. They are in for a much harder life than most. The more they know now, the better they can defend themselves in the future. Sugar coating will only cause more hardship later in life. Is that what you want for these children?"

The brutal truth rendered the Officer speechless.

"Just go easy. They lost a lot, and at Christmas, too."

But Miss Darnell held her confidence in her occupation. She would not be without the final word on the matter.

"Car accident, am I right?" Knowing already that she was, Miss Darnell did not wait for a response. "Some of these children lost their parents to a drug addict in a dark alley. Maybe I should shield them from the streets? Lock them in a room where they can live without fear? Your business is to serve and protect, and so is mine. I suggest you allow me to do my job without your judgment." Miss Darnell reached out her thin bone hands manicured by age. "I'll take the children now."

Young Sara latched onto Amy. "I don't want to stay here."

"What a shame," patronized Miss Darnell, then reached for the boy. "I am sure young Daniel here will miss you terribly."

"He doesn't want to stay here either!"

"Is that so?" Miss Darnell gasped mockingly, then turned to the boy who did not wiggle or struggle to be free from her arms, but gazed back with common sense and intelligence. "Daniel? If you would like to stay, you may help yourself to cookies and cocoa in the next room."

Confident Daniel would choose justly, Miss Darnell set him on the floor, only to be wildly deceived when he rushed to young Sara. The two children clasped onto one another.

Sara observed Miss Valentine smirk, a detail she had missed the first time.

Miss Darnell stood firm, not humiliated or embarrassed, but exhausted. She recognized the hard work which lay ahead.

"I see you two will be inseparable," realized Miss Darnell. "That will change."

Amy countered by bending down to the children's level. "Listen to me. You will find a good home with parents that will

20

more than love you; they will adore you both. I promise."

The Spirit looked to Sara once sensing her admiration for the kind lady waiver.

"I would not make promises I couldn't keep," suggested Miss Darnell.

"You will try to keep them together, Miss Darnell?" Amy pleaded.

"Of course, I will try, but as I mentioned, it will be difficult."

"Anything you can do would be appreciated."

Miss Darnell reached her hand out.

And that was the end of it. The hallway returned to its present state: the walls lost their gloss as dust clung and settled, the ceiling cracked and rained plaster, the glass lamps shattered, then faded to black. The corridor returned as it should be; the vision of yesteryear erased from sight, thus restoring the Spirit's fiery aura as the hall's only illumination. But all was not well. The palette of its flame, normally like that of a summer sunset, was not entirely as it should be. The yellow, orange, and white glow had lost some of its luster. The Spirit observed the difference at once, however subtle, while Sara was too distraught by the recent vision of her past to notice.

The Spirit's outstretched hand mimicked Miss Darnell's last image in every way, right down to its thin, nearly skeletal fingers, but Sara was not yet convinced she would take the offering.

"I was always scared of her."

"Her intentions were noble."

The Spirit listened as her mind processed its words before

she screamed, "Did you just watch what happened?! Didn't you hear her? She made me think that nobody would ever love me."

"But it was only *you* who thought nobody loved you. One did," the Spirit salvaged.

It was not without a great deal of consideration that Sara took its hand.

#

The floor dropped from under their feet, and the ceiling came down upon them. It passed through the Spirit and Sara, stopping inside another room lined with rows of bunk beds (all made) and empty, for this next vision occurred during the day. White light, as white as snow, softly entered the room from a single window at the back of the dormitory. Young Sara sat in the window sill alone as she stared down at the street below. The Spirit and Sara watched the miserable sight.

"This was the following year," proclaimed Sara, intrigued, but even more so, frightened.

The thumping of small feet came as a surprise as a three-year-old Daniel entered the room excitedly. "Hurry, Sara! Don't miss it!"

"I don't want to see this!" Sara begged, but the Spirit continued to watch without distraction.

"What's the point?" Young Sara asked, though unaware of Miss Darnell's looming presence beyond the door.

"What *is* the point?" The house mother baited, stepping inside; unintentionally capturing older Sara's attention. "Couples are not here to adopt such sad and pathetic creatures. Perhaps it is best for everybody if you stay hidden in your 'safe place'. That way, you can live here with me for the rest of your life. That must be what you want, is it not?"

Young Sara did not bite. She continued to watch the aforementioned couples park their cars and approach the front door.

"Although, it is Christmas. Prospects are typically more desperate at this time of year. You may never have a better chance."

Young Sara shifted her focus from the street to the snow-flakes that clung to the window.

"Very well. If you plan on changing your mind, I suggest you hurry. The meet and greet is only one hour."

Miss Darnell offered her hand to the boy. "Ready, Daniel?"

He gazed at the deceptively frail hand then turned to his sister at the window. Daniel made his choice by putting his hand into Miss Darnell's. She gleamed victoriously.

Sara watched her brother being led away; something she could not bring herself to do as a young girl. She wanted to scream and shake some sense into her six-year-old naïve self, but the images of the past were wiped away in a sweeping mist before she could.

Her bottom lip trembled. It took every bit of strength she had to keep from breaking.

"I didn't blame him for choosing to go with her. That whole year, all I did was hold him back. Miss Darnell was right;

nobody wanted me. And why would they? They just wanted Danny, and he never would have been adopted if they tried to keep us together. I thought I was doing the right thing."

"Your sacrifice gave your brother a chance."

Her tears broke free, but Sara continued to fight for control.

"I should have said more. I should have tried harder. His new family took him to California, and I never saw Danny again."

"Do not be so sure."

The Spirit offered its hand to Sara once again. This time, she did not waste a second to take it, desperate to learn the meaning of the Spirit's words.

#

The Spirit's radiance was not warm like before. It had dimmed more, and this time, Sara noticed. But there was no time to speak a word of it before the Spirit flew them towards the window. The frosted glass turned into that of the day's gray sky above the snow-covered sidewalk on which they stood. They had landed without physically landing.

Just ahead, two straight lines of orphans paraded in their direction. Led by a more grey-haired Miss Darnell, they marched alongside a chain-link fence that separated them from a basketball court where a group of teenage boys played.

A whistle blew. Miss Darnell's lips released the necklace whistle to shout, "Straighten those lines!"

The children had not fallen out of step. Their lines were

24

precision perfect with the exception of one, for whom the order had been meant. Being the eldest of the children, she staggered the end of the line when distracted by the boys on the court.

Sara looked upon her sixteen-year-old self with mortified reflection. Though she remembered the time well, she had forgotten about the amount of make-up she used to use (to Miss Darnell's displeasure, of course). Some layers were a form of rebellion while others were an attempt to hide her awkward complexion at an age when acne and insecurities were at their peak.

Better yet, Sara smirked at herself because she could remember choosing to ignore Miss Darnell's command.

"I said, straight, Sara!"

Teenaged Sara's watchful eyes squinted and sharpened as she turned to glare at her commander and chief.

Once Miss Darnell had each child's full attention... "When we arrive at the museum, there will be no touching. A museum is for observing, not interacting. If I see one hand touching what it should not, we will never have another field trip. Is that understood?"

The children's acknowledgment was as uniformed as their formation.

Confident in her teachings of manners and obedience, Miss Darnell turned her back to the children and continued marching them to the end of the fence. She turned the corner, falling out of Sara's sight when a boy from the court yelled, "Heads up!"

Teenaged Sara saw the basketball flying towards her head. She ducked in time, but even the safety of being a translucent vision was not enough to keep the real Sara from ducking as well. A snow bank halted the ball's escape. Teenaged Sara retrieved the toy.

The dark-haired, Latin boy of thirteen, who had called out, raced to the chain-link fence with his hands held up, ready to catch. "Throw it back!"

Teenaged Sara mocked throwing the ball over but did not let go.

Sara smiled again, accompanied by a chuckle--her first in years. "I don't know why, but I had the strongest urge to tease that boy."

The Spirit gave no response but allowed Sara to continue observing.

"What do I get if I do?" Teenaged Sara teased, playfully bouncing the ball on the concrete.

"Come on!" whined the boy. "Don't be such a girl."

"All right, I'll stop being a girl and start being a boy." She dribbled the basketball as she walked away.

"Hey! That's mine!" the boy hollered.

"Yeah? Prove it."

"It's got my name on it."

Teenaged Sara wiped off the wet mud and uncovered a name written in permanent marker. Her eyes bounced back and forth between the boy and the name.

"You don't look like a Sean to me."

"I am. Now pass it over!"

"Didn't your mother teach you any manners, Sean? What do you say?"

THE GHOST OF CHRISTMAS PAST

Another boy of lighter complexion with strands of blonde hair poking out from beneath his snow cap, yelled from the center of the court, "Hurry up!"

"Ah, come on," pleaded Sean to the girl.

"Let me hear it," she insisted.

He swallowed his pride and muttered, "Please."

Teenaged Sara hesitated before submitting. She tossed the ball over the fence towards his head. The image of him running after it reminded Sara of a dog chasing his favorite toy.

"You're welcome!" Teenaged Sara shouted before being jerked to the side by her arm clutched tightly in Miss Darnell's iron grip.

"Just what do you think you are doing, young lady?"

The Spirit and Sara watched the expression of her younger self remain as frozen as the surrounding snow.

Miss Darnell turned up Sara's mud-covered hands.

"When we arrive, you will not wash. And if I see a single fingerprint on anything in the museum, I will know precisely whom to hold responsible. Now, get back in line."

Teenaged Sara ran to catch up with the group as her elder self inquired to the Spirit, "I don't understand. Why did I need to see this part of my past?"

"Watch there." The Spirit pointed to the young boy Sara knew as Sean, who returned to the fence with the ball. Solemnly, he watched the girl and the back of an old lady, with her hair done up in a bun, disappear around the corner.

"Danny? Hey, Danny, wake up!" The blonde-haired boy shouted as he ran up.

"Danny?!" Sara muttered, aghast. She stepped away from the Spirit, and then passed through the chain-links, desperate for a closer look while the blonde boy ran up to join them.

"You know that girl or something?" But Danny reserved his answer. "Why'd you let her think you were me?"

"She might not have given me the ball if she didn't think it was mine."

"Yeah, well..." and the real Sean slapped the ball out of his Danny's hands. "It ain't yours."

Knocked from his trance, Danny raced after Sean as a mist swept in and erased the boys from sight.

"Wait! Danny!" Sara called, forgetting the rules of engagement that were bound to these passages.

The vision had finished. Sara and the Spirit returned to the brownstone's dark dormitory lit only by the apparition's light, which now burned only half as brightly. And still, Sara paid no mind. Fresh torments now haunted her, but as for the Spirit, it found this new occurrence bewitching and interfering. Never before did it have the displeasure of this experience, nor understand the reason for the fading, but the effects of its light did more than dim their surroundings. Oh, yes, so much more. The anomaly affected the knowledge it had of Sara's past: the answers there one second, then gone. In any previous moment it knew all, and then in the following, it did not, as though its gift of awareness were flipped on and off by a child playing with a switch.

"What was he doing here? He wasn't supposed to be here!" Sara hollered from behind a tear-drenched face. "Miss Darnell lied to me. Again! She told me his new parents took him far away to California. That's why we couldn't see each other no more."

Like a word on the tip of the tongue, the Spirit had a response to give, but its faltering flame refused it. Still, a reply was required. After centuries of guiding lost souls back onto their path, this eve's journey was looking to be its first failure. Hoping to avoid such a travesty, the Spirit spoke, but with some hesitancy, "Perhaps it was for the best."

Sara's rage swelled. "Whose side are you on?! I thought you were supposed to be *my* Spirit?"

"I am but a guide and do not choose sides."

"A guide?! Guide me to what? Was I supposed to be reminded of my past because everything you've showed me…I haven't forgotten? I remember it all. Why else do you think I jumped off that bridge?"

Without the knowledge gathered by its flames, the Spirit could not respond. Instead, it reached out its hand to be taken.

"Oh no!" Sara screeched. "No more. Take me back. I don't want to see anymore. Just take me back to the bridge or home or wherever; anywhere else but here."

"I do not choose the destinations. My flame decides where to take you."

"I told you I was done. It's over!"

Though she acted quickly, the Spirit would not have stopped her; the condition had been presented at journey's start. Sara swiped the nightcap from the Spirit's grip and yanked it over its brow. She continued to pull the cap down until the apparition's bare feet were covered and what of its flame remained had been extinguished.

Alone in the room, Sara turned to the third story window. The floor creaked as she stepped towards it, the first worldly noise she heard without a disorienting echo since the bridge. Yes, the Spirit of Christmas Past was gone, leaving her with pain even more trenchant than before.

#

STAVE TWO

The Christmas Angel

Should such a world exist where the Spirit would find itself inside an eternal hole as empty as black space, it would think that dimension a place of limbo between the previous Christmas time and the next. And as the Spirit examined its surroundings, illustrating the description just mentioned, it presumed such a world did truly exist, and there it stood, but with no flame to give light beyond its position.

The Spirit had no recollection of ever visiting such a timeless vacuum. In fact, as the Spirit stretched its thinking outside of this world, the journeys it had supervised were its only memories. And of all those Christmas voyages into the pasts of many condemned souls, only Sara's ended in failure. She had been different. Somehow, she had been the facilitator of this shift in phenomena.

The mist began to seep into the murky nothingness. Blemishes of darkened shadows then appeared inside the thick haze. These stains remained unrecognizable until a gap inside the rolling fog revealed a headstone, followed by another, and then another, and so on. The mist continued to thin and the Spirit discovered that every type of grave marker from every earthly era surrounded it.

The Spirit's feet were, then, anchored to the same dirt ground from which the tombstones protruded. But that was not what beheld the Spirit's attention; not in the least, for the Spirit observed the placement of an angel statue within its reach. The replica was quite hypnotic. With its extended wingspan, the width of the stone structure stretched as long as it was tall. More than that, the likeness emitted a soft, radiant glow, much like the flame the Spirit had once possessed but no longer.

A moan came from nowhere and everywhere. The Spirit dropped its attention to a curious stone slab with an unreadable inscription hidden beneath a layer of thick frost. It then turned its gaze to the engraving on the nearest plate and found it just as illegible. They all had been iced over as to keep their identity a mystery.

The next moan came from the statue. However, unlike the previous, its haunting lament spoke with innocence and hallowed beauty as it formed into a single word, "Unfortunate."

"Who are you?" the Spirit inquired.

"Unfortunate to lose such a gift," the statue repeated.

"Why have I been brought to this place?"

The Spirit received an answer in the form of a loud crack that snapped behind its back. It turned to face a headstone that had not been there previously. Unlike the others, this marker was not frosted over with ice. Instead, the placard turned into the frame of the familiar brownstone's third story window with Sara sitting on the opposite side of the glass in her "safe place." Tears streamed down her cheeks as though they were in a mad race with each other. Sara then rose, pushed open the window, and stood there without any sense or hesitation. Though Sara did not yet jump, the image implied that might be her action when the outside wall of the brownstone blurred upward while the scene fell towards the street rapidly. Before striking the bottom, the headstone returned to its previous form and displayed the inscribed:

Sara Bello

Age 43

"The woman suffers now, evermore," spoke the divine voice.

The Spirit twisted its attention back to the sculpture, only to be surprised, once again, by a real Angel where the stone figure had once stood. Her presence was glorious and magnanimous with a luminescence that burned more radiantly than any illumination the Spirit ever could cast. Her sheer gown appeared endless as tendrils of white, gossamer fabric encircled her, weaving and stitching into one another, as though guided by a gentle breeze. Her face bore such beauty as she represented joy and all that was good.

"To whom am I addressing?" the Spirit requested.

"I am an angel of Christmas, but more than that, I am your angel, your guardian, and none to any other."

The Spirit searched for any retrospect of this angel but found nothing that remotely resembled a memory. "I am not aware of your being, Angel."

"Only once your light was refused by another was my appearance essential."

"Forgive me, Angel, but I have obeyed my duty. I have broken no immortal law. Is there an offense on my part which has brought me to you?"

The Angel smiled upon the Spirit with such sweet and

35

loving admiration that it would have accepted any answer; no matter how disconcerting.

"The mortal, Sara, was misguided by your light."

"How can that be? Her grief called me to her..."

"And her subconscious filled your light with the awareness of her past, but it was you who misinterpreted that knowledge; and thereby, fortified her despair."

"Misinterpreted?"

"You could not translate what your light regarded."

The Angel's words reminded the Spirit of its flame's oddity as it depleted more and more after the conclusion of each vision. Settled that this was the correct answer to the problem, it offered the Angel, "My flame was weak. Perhaps the shadows of her past were too dark to be interpreted?"

"Dear Spirit, your flame was not weak at the start but softened as your journey with Sara progressed. Your light was leaving you already."

Knowing better than to question the Angel's authority, the Spirit inquired, "You can tell me why I was unable to interpret my flame?"

"For those souls you guide, your light holds their visions. They are a lifetime's worth; however, some visions will guide away from damnation while others will lead towards."

"You tell that Sara was not shown the proper memories which might have led her back to salvation and that I am responsible?"

"I do," claimed the Angel.

A pause was shared between them. Though the Spirit was

given a moment to search within, it was unable to see how it had erred.

"Have I not guided many souls back to their righteous paths through the ages?" the Spirit ventured. "They have reacquainted with good will, charity, and redemption. How have I succeeded with them but failed with Sara?"

"The others you speak of had much to live for. Their spectrum was broad with many hopes," explained the Angel.

"Might it be that Sara could not be saved?"

"Sara did have but a single hope."

The Spirit realized Sara's hope, as well as its own failure when it thought of her brother, Danny. "What can be done?"

"You must rekindle your flame."

"My flame is everything," confirmed the Spirit.

"It is a provision of your existence beyond your mortal life," affirmed the Angel.

"Mortal life?" The Spirit cried, repeating as though it had not heard the Angel correctly.

The Angel gazed upon the Spirit without judgment when revealing, "You do not remember because you chose to abandon your memories upon transition into this world."

A wall of silence fell between the two entities. The Spirit took a moment to search for its reflections, only to find a vacancy where memories would have been.

"I was once a human?"

"Not a long life, but a life."

"What happened?"

"That is why I have come. To rekindle your flame is to

rekindle your memories."

Though the Spirit predicted it knew the answer already, it still asked the Angel, "Where would I find my memories?"

"In your past."

Precisely as the Spirit had foreseen. To be human was to have a past, one of its own. But to have willingly abandoned memories of such a time gave the Spirit pause. It turned back to Sara's unchanged tombstone. "Tell me, Angel, have my actions doomed Sara's soul?"

"That is not for the past, for it cannot be changed, but for the future."

Then, by offering her hand, the Angel pronounced that it was time to set upon their journey, just as the Spirit had done so many times with others. It accepted her gesture, and at that moment, the Angel's spiritual ribbons danced around them in celebration.

During the disorder, one tendril saw fit to break away from the others. It wrapped itself around their held hands and sealed their grasp when the Spirit had a sudden curious thought. "Was I male or female? What was my name?"

"We shall discover all answers together."

The dancing ribbons cocooned the Spirit with the Angel then tightened into a sphere of radiance before shrinking down to the size of a distant star prior to vanishing into space.

#

Tick, tock; tick, tock; the pendulum clock repeated. The

pulses magnified within a barren, spacious ballroom with minimal furnishings to its decor. In addition to the grandfather clock, the sizable space beheld a grand harpsichord and a large marble hearth buried into the wall behind it, containing a fire that was alive and well.

To the Spirit, the room was unfamiliar, but more than that, it could not recognize the era from into which it arrived. The magnificent area rug that spread across the hardwood floor gave no clues. Its intricate design could be placed in most time periods. Much the same could be said for the crown moldings and tapestries that stretched from ceiling to floor, and covered a dozen French windows.

"I do not recognize this place. Should I start to remember something?" The Spirit inquired, sensing that it was at a disadvantage. When escorting others, they had the benefit of identifying the when and the where of their surroundings; thereby, catapulting them into their memories.

"The journey from the afterlife to the past is much longer than it is for the living, but do not despair; you will remember what is necessary once bearing witness."

"What is necessary?" The Spirit asked, puzzled.

"You will only learn what is required to find your flame."

The Angel spoke truly. Once the Spirit returned its attention to the room, memories soon caught up with its sight.

"I am beginning to remember things. I did have a life, and it was here. This was my home. I was born inside this abbey," cheered the Spirit.

The grandfather clock rang in the new hour.

"And that chime! I recognize the tone. That is the very same ring I hear when I am called to assist someone in their journey. Why is that?"

"Be still with your questions. All will be answered once you observe."

The Angel motioned towards a nearby door, but the Spirit remained elated by its memory of the clock. It noted every detail then stopped on the face, which showed the hour as being one o'clock. By the darkness outside the windows, the hour belonged to the morning.

"Can you at least tell me why I only exist within the one o'clock hour on Christmas Day?"

"Observe," the Angel insisted, repeating her gesture towards the door.

Chatter approached from the opposite side, and once the door burst open, a large crowd of Stuart men and women entered in thunderous merriment. Lords, ladies, farmers, maids; enough for a reception where status and prosperity had been denied an invitation--only to be rich in rapture did the attendant of this late night soiree need to possess.

The group hushed their exuberant gaiety forthwith, once the room's magnificent open space and high ceilings amplified their presence; however, their passion would not be deterred. And at the center of the celebration was a thoroughbred man with a drink in one hand and a cigar in the other, sharing in the same favors as the other men while the women kept smokeless and drink-less; however, no less jovial.

One elder gentleman in particular, not at all familiar to the

Spirit (yet), reached out a hand and slapped it down on the thoroughbred's brooding shoulder, "Well done, good man. A boy!"

Then, all at once, the other guests added their praise, which was met with applause from the free-handed women, making their words inaudible but no less proud.

"Thank you, Henry... everyone. Thank you for being available on such a glorious day and at such an insensible hour."

The guests chuckled at the joke ridiculously--most assuredly disorientated by the late hour.

The Spirit peered at the master of the house. Its notion of familiarity with the man intensified.

"What a blessing!" A woman concluded; finalizing the congratulatory remarks.

"Yes, thank you. No better gift could we have received on this glorious day of our Lord's birth."

"When shall we see the lad?" Henry inquired--either the master's father or a loyal friend, speculated the Spirit.

"Bethan will bring him along once Deidra is resting."

"How is Deidra? Did you speak to her?" The same woman continued as she squeezed up next to Henry.

"Fine, very fine, praise be. Bethan said the birth went smoothly this time. No worries."

"Who was worried? Not us!" A man, a stableman or yardman as he appeared more of the earth, added cheerfully.

"As I was not," then the Master quickly took a sip of his drink as a means to cover his lying lips, but the camouflage had not fooled the Spirit nor those present.

Henry returned his hand to the Master's shoulder, but

this time, as a means to console. The party halted, giving a quiet moment of observance to what must have been a tragedy yet to be spoken.

"Someone died, hadn't they?" The Spirit inquired, confused by the sudden melancholy. "Can you tell me who?"

The Angel could not. She gazed at the reenactment of the past with quiet rigor. The Spirit understood her meaning then resumed watching.

"There, now," continued Henry. "No time to mourn what has been. You have a sprite young lad that needs your full attention now."

"Right you are."

"I think this my birth," the Spirit calculated. "It would explain the day and the hour, and why the significance of the hour had followed me into the afterlife."

Henry's wife impatiently suggested, "Perhaps I should look upon them, just to be sure."

"I pray you do not, Margaret. As effortless as this birth was, I am afraid exhaustion and fatigue have demanded their moment."

And on his word, the door opened. A blustery, cheerful woman in her twenties sauntered towards the Master as the others pined for a look at the bundle held in her arms. Not yet being addressed to by name, the aforementioned mid-wife, Bethan, passed the newborn into his father's arms.

Henry wiggled his finger in front of the baby's face.

"A fine son you bore, sir." Then, the infant's tiny red hand took hold of the old man's finger. "Strong as an ox, too!"

THE GHOST OF CHRISTMAS PAST

"Henry!" Margaret bellowed, warningly. "What an unpleasant metaphor for such a charming young man."

"His name will be Morgan... Morgan the second."

The Spirit became overwhelmed by the name as it continued to remember while it learned. "That is my name then... Morgan."

"Jonathan? Jonathan?" Senior Morgan called. "Come here, boy. Introduce yourself to your new brother."

The Spirit turned to movement beneath the harpsichord and watched a somber and forlorn boy of five years crawl out from under its shadow. The connection it felt towards the boy was undeniably strong, and the Spirit knew upon that moment, "That is me. I am not the baby but that boy. I now recognize that name as being my own."

The Angel nodded her confirmation.

"Then, that must be..." the Spirit's enlightenment turned to elation "...my brother. I have a brother."

"Hurry now, Jonathan!" Morgan ordered. "Pick up your feet and come welcome Morgan Junior into his new world."

The Spirit could not remove its eyes from Jonathan as he skulked across the room.

"What is the matter? Why am I not overjoyed? I should feel no different than I do now upon learning of my new brother."

Jonathan stopped outside the crowded circle, only to be pulled into the center. Then, more carefully than handling the thinnest glass, Morgan bent down onto one knee and showed the infant Morgan to Jonathan. The brothers met with a scowl by the elder of the two boys.

"Oh, such a face!" Margaret humored. "True brothers they are indeed."

But not of any good humor as Jonathan confirmed when he spat into the infant's face.

The room fell in appalled silence until a slap boomed like cannon fire and echoed throughout the room. Once receiving a smart backhand to the face, Jonathan hit the floor.

The attending members closed in around the baby for his protection and glared down at the young monstrosity.

"Your jealousy consumed you, even before your brother's birth," spoke the Angel after a prolonged silence.

Jonathan glanced up at his father towering over him like an angry god.

Morgan ordered, "You will get up off that floor and proceed to your room, immediately."

Bethan came to Jonathan's aide and helped the boy to his feet.

"Bethan? He is not to eat or drink for all this day. He will not partake in our celebratory bounty of our Lord and Savior's birth nor the birth of his brother. He will survive only on the expectorate he so disgustingly chooses to expel." Then Morgan turned his contemptuous attention squarely onto Jonathan. "I fear word of this would break your mother's heart."

"She is not my mother," spoke the boy coldly, yet calmly.

And in a moment of weakness caused by the embarrassing actions of his son in front of those he favored, Morgan lost control of all grace. "You are right, not your real mother. You killed her."

The ballroom would have been consumed with tense

silence once again if the baby had not interrupted the uncomfortable mood with piercing wails.

Like a guard leading a criminal to his doom, the Spirit watched Bethan escort its younger self out of the room. However, for a reason quite unknown to the Spirit, she did not appear to be as revolted by Jonathan's crime. It even caught a glimpse of compassion lightening her face.

"What did my father mean that I killed my mother? How could I? Would my mortal self do such a thing?"

"Your mother died while giving you life," answered the Angel. "You never knew your mother."

The remaining memories of this incident caught up with the Spirit at that moment. "My father loved my mother terribly, didn't he? That is the motivation behind his frustration."

"So certain you are that it is your mother for whom he laments."

The Spirit did not understand what the Angel had meant. It could be construed that there had been another family member who did not survive long enough to be a part of this shadow. *A sister perhaps?*

Drawn by cries, the Spirit released all thoughts on the matter and stepped through the once gleeful crowd, now more like a lynch mob, and gazed upon the infant as Jonathan should have done all these many years ago.

"All will be fine come morning," assured Margaret's voice of reason.

"And how, pray tell, do you know this?" Morgan asked, amused.

"I am a mother, do not forget. Mothers know these things. Jonathan's a strong boy, made of thick skin…like his father."

Morgan smiled; a silent, *thank you.* He passed the infant into Margaret's arms, and in doing so, the woman gleamed with joy. The newborn continued to command attention from the others, allowing Morgan to slip away and stare out a nearby window.

The Spirit followed the man who once had been his father and stopped at his side. "He is regretting his actions, is he not?"

"He is," the Angel confirmed.

"I was not present to see his shame. How could I have known otherwise?"

"It would not have mattered. You would not have believed in your father's love for you, even if he could have expressed it."

The Spirit observed the man closely, and silently. "I regret too. The jealousy I carried for my brother was misguided."

"And what of your jealousy?" The Angel quizzed.

"My father did not honor me, his firstborn son, with his name, but chose to give it to his second born."

Sunlight pierced through the frosted window. Its essence burned bright, but this light was not of the earth. The beam did not highlight Morgan but made him vanish from the Spirit's sight. The Angel had brought forth the morn of a new shadow.

#

The fire in the hearth could inspire something of a circus performance: the flame's lion-like roar accompanied the log's popping sap as it snapped like a tamer's whip. Yet, the loud crackling could not deter from pounding footsteps that clambered from the adjacent hall.

A three-year-old Morgan raced into the ballroom through the door that had been left perched open. The Spirit and the Angel watched the exceedingly cheerful child, who had not yet reached an age when life's burdens weighed upon his shoulders, race up to the Spirit then stop and peer directly into the its eyes to bless, "Happy Christmas!"

For a brief moment, the Spirit had forgotten the shadow he had been presented, mistaking it for real time when it returned a smile.

"Happy Christmas, to you Morgan," spoke a voice from behind.

The Spirit turned to discover that its terrestrial father had been positioned at its back. Morgan Senior bent down to pick up his son, reaching through the Spirit when doing so.

"And a Happy Birthday to you, as well," continued Morgan. "Where is your brother? Has Jonathan not yet awoken?"

But little Morgan had been distracted by a hard lump in his father's vest and patted the pocket.

"What's that? Is it for me?" The child gleamed.

"What would give you the impression that I would have anything for you on your birthday, and on Christmas Day, no less?"

Though the elder of the two Morgan's appeared amused by his shenanigans, the excited junior Morgan was not. "Can I see?!"

"Clever you are, but we must wait until Jonathan arrives before presenting gifts."

Another pair of running feet, heavier than the previous, turned everyone's attention to the door to watch a handsome woman barrel into the room, and out of breath.

"Jonathan is missing!" The woman cried, beside herself.

In the moment of silence that followed, the Spirit's memory of Deidra was revived.

"My step-mother," the Spirit confirmed as it gazed at her admiringly. "I had never known a more kind soul, and yet somehow, I had found a way to dislike her."

"Do not dwell on your shame, Spirit. She is not this shadow's intended."

Heeding the Angel's instruction, the Spirit resumed its concentration on the unfolding scene.

"He's not in his room or in the yards or barn, or any other room," panicked Deidra. "I have searched them all."

"Obviously not all because he is still in hiding," seethed Morgan then handed their son over in preparation to take it upon himself to look.

He made it as far as the door when Deidra called, "Morgan?! Be gentle. It's Christmas."

Morgan stopped. He turned methodically. "Right you are. It is Christmas. It's a time to celebrate and rejoice; not to succumb to the trappings of a bitter, cold child."

"Our son is neither bitter nor cold," she demanded.

"Correct. *Our* son is not. *My* son is."

Deidra's appalled reaction came as a surprise to the

48

Spirit, which did not improve its spirit, but rather, heightened the consuming guilt it had towards the woman.

"What dare say you?"

"Jonathan does not deserve your motherly love. I am apologizing to have burdened you with such a responsibility."

At that moment, the Spirit recalled hearing those exact words. It turned away from the chaotic scene and focused on a lump behind a drapery. "There I was…this whole time."

With a face flushed bright red with anger, Deidra handed little Morgan back to the scoundrel.

"The only burden I bear is the wretchedness of your fatherhood." She stormed out of the room to resume her search without her husband's assistance.

The Spirit witnessed Morgan hug his youngest boy tightly. The embrace melted their father's hardened demeanor and put a smile on his face. A grain of that centuries old jealousy returned. The Spirit peered back at the lump in the curtain.

"Would you like to see your gift now?" Morgan inquired cheerfully, as though the day had been refreshed.

Any doubters who would think the boy would decline the invitation would be proven the fool when little Morgan responded with firm, jerking nods that threw Morgan Senior off his balance. The man laughed heartily. "Are you sure? It's my special gift, made just for you."

"Yes, father. Please!"

"You may reach into my vest pocket, but only if you are sure that…"

Young Morgan had his hand dug inside the coat before

allowing his father to finish. What he pulled out was a hand-whittled piece of wood containing six intricately placed holes. Nonetheless thrilled, the boy raised an eyebrow to the gift. "What is it, father?"

"I will show you," and with that, set his son on his feet to hold the flute to his lips. He inhaled a deep breath then began to play a lively tune. The demonstration had continued for only a moment before Deidra's accompanying cries for Jonathan in the background were an unwelcomed addition to the, otherwise, sweet symphony.

Morgan handed the flute back to his son. The boy beamed at the gift then gave his best effort to mimic the music his father created, only to succeed in making a noise best left in the company of unconditional loved ones.

Morgan chuckled before comforting, "Give it time. I will teach you to play better than I ever could."

"What about Jonathan?" The boy probed.

The father had calmed at the mention of his eldest son's name. He suggested, "I think Jonathan may wish for us to find him hiding. Shall we look together?"

Young Morgan nodded enthusiastically. But before joining Deidra in Jonathan's game of hide and seek, their father took the flute from his son and placed it on the hearth's mantel.

Once the two exited, the lump in the curtain stirred, and an eight-year-old Jonathan emerged. Carefully, and most quietly, he approached the hearth, and with the help of the glow from the whipping flames, the Spirit saw the glistening tears streaming down Jonathan's cheeks. The condition of its former self did not come as a shock.

While young Morgan's distant calls echoed in the hall beyond the room, Jonathan removed the flute from the mantle and put one end to his mouth. Then, as though the instrument had bitten him on his lips, he threw the viper-like pipe into the fire.

"I knew it!" Morgan spat under tempered fury. He not only startled the boy but the Spirit as well as the delay in recalling this memory, or any other, continued.

Jonathan backed into the harpsichord as Morgan stomped his advance. He reached into his vest pocket and produced another flute; identical to the one disintegrating in the hearth.

"I'll be giving Morgan this one. You just burnt yours."

Morgan placed the pipe in the exact spot on the mantel where its twin had rested. He turned to his frightened boy and leered.

"I'm sorry father. I didn't mean it. Please!"

Though the mask of anger Morgan wore upon his face foretold his mood, his eruption still came as a surprise to both Jonathan and the Spirit when taking his son by the ear and tugging him towards the hall. And though they vanished behind the wall, the ballroom continued to swell with the echoes of Jonathan's cries.

The Spirit turned to the flute that continued to haunt. "He could not see that my actions were but a cry for his love."

"Just as you could not see his love for you," the Angel pointed out calmly.

"If he had loved me, should he not have presented this gift just as he did to my brother?"

"Your father was not without fault. Try as he did, you were more important to him than even he could realize."

"Then why did he act as though he despised me so?"

As the Spirit waited for the Angel's reply, the only image it had known of her transformed into Deidra; however, when she spoke next, the Angel retained her unearthly tone, "I am not Morgan's one true love."

"He continued to blame me for my mother." The Spirit realized.

The Angel returned to her white brilliance form. "You were a constant reminder of her life...and her death."

The Spirit turned to the pipe and obeyed its desire to reach for it though knowing he could not touch. "Tormenting are these memories."

"And though your remorse is misplaced, you are now closer to finding your flame."

Confused, the Spirit inquired, "What do you mean, 'misplaced'?"

"You were very much like your father. Just as his love for you escaped him, so did your love for another."

The Angel's ribbons fluttered and danced identical to before, and once again, a single luminescent tendril broke away from the cluster. But with no held hand to wrap around for a second time, it covered the Spirit's eyes. Instead of darkness, the Spirit was blinded by white light.

#

The Ghost of Christmas Past

The Angel's ribbon released its grip. Upon its new sight, the Spirit distinguished little difference as to the whereabouts of its next vision. In place of the endless white brilliance was an endless dull gray that surrounded them; however, the atmosphere's new rhythmic harmony was noted. A chorus of geese, heron, bitterns, cranes, and pheasant replaced the snaps and roars of the hearth's healthy fire.

But the Spirit did not enjoy the wilderness's orchestration welcoming a new day when its concentration was held captive. The Spirit required further information before relinquishing itself to the next segment.

"This other you spoke of, who Jonathan hid his love for, would it be Morgan, my brother?"

"It would be."

The Spirit then cast its full attention upon its environment. The idea that the Angel would deliver such a conclusion, and then bring it to place where nothing could be observed, was bewildering. But as the Spirit centered its concentration on the gray density, the mass began to stir. The shadows of tall trees came into view between the breaks. The Spirit learned that it had been brought to a forest doused by early morning's fog.

"This is strange," affirmed the Spirit. "Am I right to think that spending Christmas morning in such a dismal place was peculiar?" Though before the Angel might have replied, the sound of approaching gallops disrupted nature's song.

Two horses, and their riders, sliced through the murky haze. The Spirit recognized each driver despite them speeding past. Both Jonathan and young Morgan looked to have aged

53

to twelve and seven respectively, prime ages to take part in a dangerous race such as this.

"Faster, Morgan, Faster," taunted Jonathan, in the lead by mere feet.

"I'm catching up!" Morgan warned.

Then, from the place where the boys had emerged, Deidra's voice followed, "Don't go too deep!"

"And stay clear of the lake," added Morgan Senior as the two halted next to the Spirit and the Angel.

The Spirit remembered, "This was our new Christmas tradition. It was our family outing before any celebration."

Giddy at hearing their two sons enjoying each other's company, Deidra suggested, "I don't think they heard us."

"I do believe we have lost them," spoke Morgan, equally jovial.

The Angel interrupted the moment to insist, "Come." Then, at the speed of twenty horses, she and the Spirit rushed through the forest. They did not dodge a single tree or bush but glided through any obstruction to arrive at Jonathan's side.

"You'll never beat me!" The boy cheered. "I'll always be older and faster."

Young Morgan slapped the reins, dodging low branches, logs, and rocks as he sped faster. And the more the gap between the two boys decreased, the more Jonathan's playful disposition soured. There could be no missing the gleaming determination in the boy's face.

He came upon a wall of wild shrubs. Jonathan waited until the right moment to veer onto the opposite side. Morgan could not react fast enough and separated from his brother, who then veered at an angle and disappeared in the mist. Morgan cried foul while Jonathan's laughter echoed provokingly, having no choice but to ride alongside the full length of the shrubs before pivoting around the barrier.

Under the Angel's guidance, the Spirit was not given a choice as to which rider to follow. It flew steadily at Jonathan's side, looking back into mist, now and again, worried to see any shadow of little Morgan.

It saw none.

Jonathan roared maniacal laughter in the Spirit's ear--a flagrant attempt to egg his brother--though the reproach had worked as a beacon once Morgan's voice cried from somewhere near, "Wait for me!"

Jonathan pulled on the reins. His mount came to a stop then he hollered in kind, "I told you, you couldn't keep up!"

But the Spirit experienced no relief. Though its memory of this shadow had yet to be realized, it did recall this forest and all of the dangers that lurked from old downed logs that camouflaged in the fog to scattered brush too large to see what lay on the opposite side. The Spirit became distressed at the idea that Morgan could become more lost with each passing moment.

It turned to make an inquiry to the Angel, but instead, the Spirit gazed upon a vague shadow of her existence in the distance. "Angel? What is there that I need to witness?"

Her image did not speak back nor move in the slightest, and even more remarkable than her mystery, was Jonathan's ability to witness her as well.

55

From atop his mount, the boy paused at the Spirit's side when catching sight of the dark silhouette looming in the mist. He questioned its existence with a kindly, "Hello?"

But the image, which easily might be perceived as the Angel of Death, did not respond…and perceived as such it was when the sounds of splashing water accompanied young Morgan's pleas for help.

Like mirrored complexions, Jonathan and the Spirit ignored the ominous image and darted their gazes in the direction of the distressed cries.

Jonathan snapped the reins and hollered his horse to charge. He followed the rising volume of the boy's cries in sync with panicked splashing to a rider-less horse stationed on the top of a small drop-off.

Upon the sight of Morgan drowning in a marsh, the Spirit was released from its counterpart's side. It swooped down the muddy cascade and soared into a position above the boy. Fear filled the Spirit so much so that in a moment of desperation, it ignored the barriers between their paralleled worlds and cried Jonathan to hurry.

Morgan went under, as though panic had placed its hand upon his head and pushed.

"No! Come back!" The Spirit pleaded.

At first, one might consider what happened next to be a miracle of the day when Morgan's head lifted above the surface upon the plea, only to then extend an arm as he looked into the Spirit's eyes to beg, "Please! Help me!"

The Spirit reached without thought and passed its hand

56

through Morgan's; experiencing not even the slightest sensation of touch. It tried again, hoping the first attempt was in error, but nothing changed.

"Please, Lord, no!" The Spirit beseeched.

"Take my hand! Jonathan!" Morgan implored before his head fell below the surface, and did not come back up for air as it had before.

The Spirit twisted to find Jonathan frozen at the water's edge, standing stiff as cold stone since his arrival. Of course, it was he whom Morgan had pleaded to and reached for. What initially was thought to have been a Christmas miracle had been unreal. The rules of the universe remained absolute.

Jonathan did nothing but watch his brother struggle. His stone-like stare kept as still as a mountain's face. Indicative of their father, the Spirit had a sudden inclination to expel many choice words at the boy, when calls from his father in the near distance snapped the boy from his trance.

Jonathan hollered, "Down here," before grasping a branch with one hand and leaping into the marsh. He extended his free hand and dug below the water's surface.

Morgan Senior reached the hilltop in time to witness Jonathan pull young Morgan's coughing head above water. He slid down the slope and wasted no time to wrap his boys safely inside his arms, smothering them both with affection.

"Thank you, Jonathan. God bless you, my son."

The Spirit witnessed the spectacle that was celebrating a false hero.

"Now I see why I left my memories behind," spoke the

Spirit. "I did not want to remember the person I was."

"Do you not yet realize all this shadow offers?" The Angel's voice asked.

"I do," admitted the Spirit, distracted by Deidra's arrival onto the scene. Her hysterical relief augmented the spectacular display of love for one another. "If you refer to the thoughts Jonathan had while watching his brother struggle, I do remember what spell I was cast under."

"Then you realize malice was not in your heart."

"But anyone who might have witnessed my hesitation would have believed otherwise. They would have perceived the worst kind of villain, as I had."

"There was no wrongdoing in visualizing a world your brother had never been born into. Imagination is human."

The Spirit turned to face its mentor but did not find her at its side. Her presence eluded the Spirit for a moment until finding her in the lake's reflection, waiting inside the abbey--no doubt, the destination of their next vision.

The Spirit addressed the likeness, "My hesitation was my wrongdoing. I had allowed my jealousy to consume me and put Morgan's well-being into danger's custody. I now know why I left my memories behind." The Spirit then gazed sharply at the Angel to make sure its wish was made clear. "I cannot go on with this knowledge. Please rid me again of these memories."

"Impossible," refused the Angel.

"Then what point was there to having them discarded if it were only meant to be temporary?" The Spirit demanded under mounting frustration. "Might these conditions have been presented at the time of my choosing? Or did I refuse the memory of that option too?"

Though the Angel remained unaffected by the Spirit's mutiny, she warned, "Challenge if you must, but do not abandon the search for your light. Sara's soul is dependent upon your success."

Collecting its conduct, the Spirit returned to a calm state. There was no question as to Sara's soul hanging in limbo, but what the Spirit was quick to remind was, "She is for the future. Is that not what you stated?"

"Indeed," she replied pleasantly, and then stretched her hand towards the Spirit. Her luminescent arm broke the water's surface and reached for the taking.

"What other consequences might I face for abandoning this journey?"

"The only path I know is this. What lay beyond my offering is unknown to me."

The focus on her hand intensified as the Spirit pondered potential ramifications. There were many to consider including interminable purgatory, as well as dissension for its crimes as a human, both learned and unlearnt. On the upside, ascension for services rendered, while a spirit, might be a possibility.

"The choice must be yours," continued the Angel.

No other verdict could have born more weight, but that did not trouble the Spirit as it made its decision posthaste. "I refuse."

So there it was; the choice made.

The Angel withdrew her hand back into the water. Her

radiant bloom then faded and took with her the background image of the abbey's interior walls, as well as the family rejoicing on the marsh's edge.

The Spirit had been left alone in the forest. And at the moment after it wondered whether it would roam these woods for all eternity, the Spirit's focus was drawn back to the lake. As it should, the water's surface did not reflect the treetops and sky. Instead, the lake looked to be filled with tar; its black surface reminded the Spirit of the netherworld it visited between Sara's journey and its own.

A twig snapped from beyond the trees. The Spirit spun around. The rolling mist continued to make seeing anything beyond fifty feet ahead difficult. There was no telling the cause of the disruption. On many occasions, while living as Jonathan, the Spirit was sure he had been frightened, but none would compare to the fear now experienced.

Next came a splash. Its taunt was too gripping for the Spirit to ignore. It turned back towards the lake of black muck that now surged and waved as though the ground had shaken the substance to life. But as unexpected as the lake's form appeared to the Spirit, the anomaly held no weight compared to the skeletal hand that broke through the surface and reached towards the Spirit. The colorless and thin thing halted its stately presence once close enough to touch.

Whereas anyone else would have run, the Spirit accepted the ghoulish offering instantly for it knew there would be conse-quences when refusing to continue its memories; however, the Spirit certainly did not expect what was presented.

THE GHOST OF CHRISTMAS PAST

Where the Angel's ribbons had been white and inviting, the ribbons that emerged from the lake were black and mysterious. They tangled around the Spirit then drew it to the surface, submerging it beneath the deep of its folds.

#

STAVE THREE

The Other Spirits

Not sludge; fabric. That had been the black substance which consumed the Spirit. But only once the material parted like draperies did the Spirit realize the component.

The inky cloth continued to fold into itself until taking the form of a hooded figure positioned at the Spirit's side. Its garments concealed all beneath it, all but the lingering hand. The Spirit stared at the ominous Phantom, recognizing it without introduction.

"I know you, or of you, at least. I never considered our meeting a possibility; I of the past and you of the future."

The Ghost of Christmas Yet-To-Come stood erect and majestic, neither confirming nor denying the Spirit's statement.

"Why have you come for me?"

The deadened silence had been present ever since arriving at their location though the Spirit only came to realize the absence of noise while awaiting the Phantom's response, which never came.

"You have no dialogue because the future has to be written," realized the Spirit.

The Phantom nodded its affirmation before lifting a bony finger and pointing to the bright corridor which they occupied.

The sterile passageway was unfamiliar to the Spirit. Its walls and floor gleamed with a metallic luminosity behind moving images in picture frames. The floor beneath the Spirit's position differed only in that there were no moving pictures. The Spirit came to realize that it had been transported to a time in which it had never visited…or at least, remembered visiting.

It moved towards the closest digital image of an early twentieth-century snow scene. Inside the frame, a small man and his young son dragged a freshly cut pine tree towards a cabin house with light glowing warmly through its windows. The image then repeated itself. The Spirit turned to another frame hanging on the adjacent wall. Ice skaters twirled and glided below a magnificently large Christmas tree in Rockefeller Plaza, New York. Though the year the Phantom had brought it to was unfamiliar, the Spirit deduced these images played because the day was Christmas.

A highly advanced and technical machine beeped at the Spirit's side suddenly. Next to the instrument rested an unused gurney.

"A hospital?" It questioned.

The Phantom did not need to affirm the Spirit's inquiry when uniformed staff suddenly bustled in and out of adjacent dormitories, giving this image life. However, the one room the Phantom had positioned them in front of remained undisturbed. It pointed, and the Spirit faced the closed door.

Before entering, the Spirit attempted to prepare for what mystery lay beyond, but deciphering the unknown was impossible without even a hint as to what type of errand the Ghost of Christmas Future had been charged to guide. Whatever it may be, the Spirit suspected the shadow would be difficult to observe. In its past experiences of escorting troubled souls to memories of hospitals, they rarely provided a merry outcome.

The Ghost of Christmas Past

But regardless of any trepidation, the Spirit did as instructed.

The door did not need to open. The pair moved through and stopped amongst an assembly of loved ones, grieving and sobbing over Mary, the bedridden woman in her final moments.

"Where's David? Is he here yet?" Mary asked.

Her husband, Ben, who struggled to hold back his tears while holding her hand and responding, "Not yet, Mary. He's on his way."

Mary smiled and rested her worry.

Although the Spirit was unacquainted with this particular shadow, it assumed, quite confidently, that this image had been intended for a man named David; yet, there were no other ghostly observers present.

"Where is David?" The Spirit asked in hopes that the Phantom might point him out in the gathering, but it did not. "Is he not here because I am not?"

The Phantom gave no response of any kind; not a single movement. It continued to look upon the scene as though to suggest the Spirit do the same.

"Did David arrive?" Mary repeated.

"Not yet, my darling," repeated Ben as well, "but he's coming. Just hold on a bit longer."

Mary smiled again. "I will."

The Spirit asked, "Is David but only one of many who will suffer his consequences without my existence? Is that what you came to show me? How the needs of others will not be fulfilled without my light to guide them?"

67

But the Phantom did not entertain the query; not even to twitch its festering finger. It kept as still as the deathly air that encompassed all in the room.

"David needs to bear witness," continued the Spirit. "Otherwise, his spirit will be burdened for all eternity."

"Where's David?" Mary asked, as though asking for the first time. "Is he here yet?"

"Not yet, my darling. Soon," answered Ben, continuing to do his best to show no misgiving. "Just keep holding on. He'll be here, my love."

Though Mary smiled, the subtext of her remorse was plain. She gazed at those who surrounded her and wept during her moment of lucidity. It had become evident... "David's not coming."

Mary turned to her husband, still holding her hand, to request, "Tell our son that I will always be with him. I'm moving on to become his guardian angel."

Mary closed her eyes. They stayed closed.

The somberness inside the room spiraled. Woeful cries came from all who had witnessed Mary's last moment. The Spirit exercised its strength to keep from joining their lament; not only for her soul but David's too, for his absence from this vision could be his doom.

"There is an odd familiarity about this image," realized the Spirit suddenly. "Not that I have witnessed this scene before, I know that it has yet to occur, but it appears all loved ones knew of Mary's condition, and yet, David's absence is the only one noticed. Was that by his choice?"

The Ghost of Christmas Past

The Phantom nodded graciously, affirming what the Spirit had suspected.

"Then David is much like Jonathan. Both care only for their self-interest."

The Spirit's statement went unconfirmed by the Phantom though it required no endorsement. The truth was in the familiarity.

The shadow did not fade away but continued to haunt the Spirit as it stated disapprovingly, "Any number of future shadows could have been demonstrated to show the effects of my absence, but you have chosen this one in particular. It appears you and the Angel have invented a way to refuse what I demanded and kept me in my learning." Nothing came of the Spirit's egging. The Phantom gave no indication and continued its resolve. "The world is filled with kinder, more deserving people than I to fill the role of Christmas Past. Surely, there must be one more worthy to hold my position."

Something the Spirit said surrendered the moment because the Phantom's robes suddenly whipped and fluttered in the space around them until all was erased. What triggered such an unnerving presentation, the Spirit did not know. All that remained in such a black void was the Phantom's single white finger. It pointed in the direction for the Spirit to walk.

#

The darkness lingered into the next vision that occurred at night. What amount of modest light did pierce the bleakness coming through a single window, though insufficient enough for the Spirit to distinguish its whereabouts or the year in which the Phantom had transported them.

The obscurity lasted no longer than the count of ten before the Spirit and the Phantom were joined by a second pair of observers, doused in a harmless white flame. They stood just feet away inside a cramped, dilapidated living room. Instead of trading bewildered gazes with the Spirit and the Phantom, the pudgy man of sixty and a little girl of ten analyzed the dreaded conditions of where they stood, none the wiser to the other spectral presences.

The girl was a spirit as well; that was apparent. In addition to the unburning radiance, it bore a white tunic while holding a snuffer in one hand and wearing a wreath of holly that crowned its head. Until this night, much about this apparition had likened the Spirit.

"The little girl is the Ghost of Christmas Past who will replace me?"

The Phantom nodded.

The man accompanying the new Ghost was unfamiliar to the Spirit, though by the nametag he bore on his snug police uniform, it knew his surname to be O'Reilly.

The officer gave no effort to hide his distaste for the meager conditions in which they stood. He glared at a floral print sofa, no longer vibrant with colors that were once pink, yellow, and white, but now earth-toned. The walnut coffee table was just as much of an eye-sore with multiple water rings on the surface and scratches too deep to be buffed. It rested directly across from a battered entertainment center displaying kitsch knickknacks and figurines that surrounded a large television with a crack down the center of its screen.

O'Reilly growled, "Where are we? What am I doin' in this pit? What's this got to do with me?"

"You will see there," the Ghost responded in a voice as pleasant as a chord of sweet symphonic music while pointing towards a kitchen scarcely grazed by its light.

The Spirit did not follow the other Ghost's gesture, but instead, marveled at its presence. "The soul of this Ghost of Christmas Past seems very young." The statement was meant to be rhetorical. The Phantom was not expected to give input, but even if it were so inclined to nod or indicate, the distraction of a tired and poorly woman in her forties, appearing where the other Ghost had indicated, would not have allowed it.

A flashlight helped guide Stella Newcomb through the dark. Draped around her thin shoulders was a handcrafted shawl over layers of sweaters attempting to keep her warm. Her breath disintegrated after leaving a misty trail as she passed the entertainment center and entered the kitchen. Stella picked up the tea kettle next to the sink then placed it under the faucet and twisted the knob.

"No! No! No!" She cried, uniformly banging the spout each time she aired her grievance.

O'Reilly chuckled at the woman's misfortune. "Her pipes are frozen."

"No," corrected the other Ghost. "Like her electricity, she could not afford what was owed."

O'Reilly stopped cackling then continued to watch Stella's hardship with noticeable boredom. "Who is she anyway? I don't know her."

"But you know her son."

The front door opened. A young man of twenty years entered quietly, though not quietly enough.

"Andy?" Stella called from the kitchen.

"Yeah, ma," he answered, making a beeline for the hallway, emitting an involuntary moan with each step. Andy's attempt to exit the living room unseen failed when Stella's flashlight beamed his face, as well as a large gash above his brow.

Again, O'Reilly chuckled. "You're right. Him I know. He's a no good punk. Doing eight upstate for armed robbery."

The clank of the tea kettle striking the floor echoed deafeningly. Stella darted to her son, crying, "Andy! What happened?" while reaching towards the wound that had been crusted over with frozen blood. Despite her gentleness, Andy hissed like a gas leak and jolted his head back.

Stella guided him to the sofa. "You promised me no more fighting."

"I wasn't the one fighting," he explained with controlled anger.

"Who did this?"

"Honest, Mom, I was just walking home."

"Tell me, Andy," ordered Stella, as she reached to press the edge of her sweater's sleeve onto the gash.

Again, Andy pulled away. He asked, "Don't you need something wet to clean the blood?"

Stella lowered her arm. She hesitated before confessing,

THE GHOST OF CHRISTMAS PAST

"I'm sorry, baby. Water's been shut off. I thought I paid them enough. I honestly did."

His eyes did not accuse, nor did his tone give blame when he replied, "It's okay, momma."

"Now, tell me who did this to you, baby," begged Stella.

Andy's humble demeanor turned sour. "The police! Who else?" He raged, slipping back into uncontrolled anger that now fought back.

"But why?"

The other Ghost looked to the remorseless man at its side. No one present doubted that he was the one responsible for Andy's condition.

O'Reilly fidgeted under the Ghost's weighted stare. Then, as though realizing there was no escape, he blared, "He deserved it! The kid resisted!"

"He said I attacked some old lady for her purse," blamed Andy. "But I didn't! You know I wouldn't hurt no one like that."

"Yeah, I know that, baby," comforted Stella, patting her son's hand reassuringly. "I raised you better than that."

Uncomfortable silence took over the image. The Ghost utilized the moment to confirm, "He was not guilty of that crime."

"Maybe not that one," asserted O'Reilly. "But he still broke the law. When a cop yells 'stop,' you don't keep running. It ain't my fault if he looks like the perp described. Besides, it was only a matter of time. All you gotta do is look at him to know that. Look how they live! I tried to help the kid by beating a little sense into him."

The other Ghost did not challenge O'Reilly's position.

The warping of Andy's face, as he rose from the sofa, demonstrated the pain he tolerated from unnoticeable injuries.

"What are you doing? Sit back down!" Stella cried. "I need to take care of you."

But Andy proceeded to a coat closet by the front door as a sleepwalker under the spell of his subconscious would do.

Stella watched her son, confused and frightened. "What are you doing?"

Andy retrieved a revolver from the top shelf. "It's Christmas, Momma. I need to take care of you, too, and get what's ours. I'm gonna make sure we at least got water."

Andy disappeared from the vision when he stepped out of the room. Stella and her cries vanished as well when she chased after him.

"See!" O'Reilly bellowed. "What did I tell you? I'm never wrong. The punk's going to go rob that convenience store and shoot the clerk."

"Andy was driven by fear and desperation," amended the Ghost.

"So? That doesn't matter! The law's the law. And what he did has got nothing to do with me. So I shoved the kid around a little. Big deal! I didn't put the gun in his hand. I had nothing to do with who he already was. He's a criminal!"

"Is it a criminal whom you think Stella raised?"

"You know what? I don't like your allegations, and I don't like you. I've had enough of this." And in an instant, O'Reilly swiped the nightcap from the Ghost's hand and doused its flame, but not without exclaiming, "Go hassle someone else!"

The Ghost of Christmas Past

O'Reilly faded from the scene that had reached its conclusion.

The snuffing of the other Ghost's flame had been just as quick as what the Spirit remembered when Sara extinguished its own. It declared to the Phantom, "Even as spirits, we are imperfect. My replacement will not address how O'Reilly's actions were the catalyst for Andy's downfall. The Ghost will not know how to interpret this shadow's meaning. Is that because of her age?" The Spirit waited but a moment for a response of any kind. When one did not come, it continued, "How could such a young soul be chosen as my replacement? I was young too, when Jonathan, but not so young. How are we chosen?" It paused again. The Spirit grew more frustrated by its continued silence. "Though I realize now this shadow's purpose was to show that any misguidance can occur no matter the spirit, I fear it has only raised more questions than answers. I still am not convinced to return to my journey."

The Future's robe separated into those ribbons that were familiar. They wove through the air towards the Spirit to cloak it inside a black bubble.

#

The bubble burst, and the remains dissipated. Not only had the Spirit been returned to the orphanage dormitory but to the very spot where its flame had been extinguished. It searched for the mysterious Phantom, but the specter kept its whereabouts unknown, though when scanning its immediate area, the Spirit did note that it was not alone.

Sara sat in front of the open third story window, sniffling and moaning in her 'safe place.' Immediately, the situation reminded the Spirit of the scene it had watched performed at the cemetery's tombstone when shown Sara leaping to her death. That display had been horrid to watch, and the Spirit was pleased to see Sara sitting inside the building and not laying outside.

"Phantom? Why have I returned to this place?" The Spirit asked in hopes of luring out the Ghost of Christmas Future, despite knowing full well that the specter would not articulate a reply but perhaps communicate with a pointing of its bony finger.

"Calm your despair," the Spirit's voice spoke...only these words never leaped off the Spirit's tongue. In fact, it had not even considered such a statement.

"What are you doing here? I thought I got rid of you," spat Sara, and then hurled the very same nightcap she had used to extinguish the Spirit's flame at its feet. A mysterious clank accompanied her action, but the bereft tune went unnoticed while Sara continued to aggress, "A lot of good that did."

Impossible! And yet somehow, someway, this shadow appeared to have bent the rules of the universe and allowed Sara to communicate with what should be unknown to her senses.

The past and the present cannot interact. Impossible, repeated the Spirit in silence before remembering the incident at the lake, and how it had believed that young Morgan reached out to the Spirit for help when, in fact, he had reached for Jonathan standing on the shore behind it. The cause for that deception had been simply where the Spirit was positioned, and on that thought, it stepped to the side and found an exact replica of itself inside the room.

The two spirits were identical in every way, right down to the white tunic and gray hair long enough to sweep the dusty floor.

Meanwhile, Sara continued her assault, "What's the point of putting out your fire if you're only gonna come back?"

"Though you are no longer by my side, it is my future which I continue to observe," addressed the Spirit to the unseen Phantom, while watching its double bend to retrieve the nightcap. "Not as Jonathan but as the spirit I've become. That is how Sara is able to interact with me. This is my future, but then..."

"Where is your fire?" Sara inquired as though speaking on the Spirit's behalf, calling attention to the missing component both spirits shared. "How come I can see you without it?"

"It will not return to me," the Future Spirit explained.

Stunned by the clarification, Sara rose to her feet.

Clank Clink Clang. The offensive noise did not escape Sara a second time. She discovered her wrists bound by chains when lifting her arms. Mortified, Sara gaped at the heavy shackles. "What are these?"

"Chains forged in life; link by link," answered the Future Spirit.

Sara shrilled, "In life? You mean I'm dead?"

The Spirit floated to the open window that hung like a portrait on the wall with nothing but gray on its canvas. Every brownstone and street lamp and skyscraper from earlier had been removed from the background. But before peering down, it looked back at the Future Spirit who stayed its position.

"I know what I will find. I have already seen this," realized the Spirit.

It had no intention of dismantling the timeline. Keeping the universe on course to this future trajectory, the Spirit peered through the frame, along with Sara, to discover her mortal body lying across the stoop below.

Rattling chains and woeful moaning followed when Sara drifted away from the window in unparalleled horror.

"I jumped?" She exclaimed. "But I...I don't remember jumping."

Knowing all too well, the Future Spirit offered, "In the transition from life, memories can be discarded."

The incessant rattling overpowered her next moan. Sara struggled to lift the heavy irons, "But how did I get these?"

"The links are your self-pity coupled by links of your regrets. They strand together to form a suicide's anchor."

"Anchor?!" Sara shouted, horrified. "What's that supposed to mean? Like trapped? I'm trapped here?"

"This is your home."

"It's *not* my home!" She cried before rising into the air and soaring towards the opening, but her endeavor to escape proved futile when the bindings tightened and kept her a nose's length from freedom. Sara screeched at her defeat and filled the space with wails of a mournful banshee.

"There is nothing to be done. You are in judgment."

"You did this to me!" Sara accused angrily.

"It was not your time. You were not ready."

"I was ready! I was ready until you gave me hope. I thought I lost my brother forever, but then you showed me how close we had come to finding each other. You showed me reasons to regret my life and pity myself. That's what you said these chains were, right? Before you, all I wanted was to end my pain, but now you made it last forever."

The chains of remorse scraped the floor as Sara returned to her 'safe place' and cried for the lost brother who continued to live in a separate world.

The Spirit observed its Future self befuddled...beaten... lost, who watched Sara continue to wallow in despair.

"Oh, now I see. Sara's torture is to be my own. She is meant to haunt me for eternity. Because of my failures, I will be damned to share her purgatory."

Should silence be considered a deliverable sound, then that was what the other side replied. However, the absence of any verbal communication did not dampen the Spirit's resolve further but, in fact, elevated its perception of its situation.

It transferred focus onto Sara. "We have indeed led paralleled lives. Her emptiness reminds me of the isolation Jonathan felt in life. Perhaps being raised with a lack of affection, as well as the regrets we share for a brother, is what binds us, and why, without my memories, my light could not empathize with her torments. Though I now wish I had continued my quest to rekindle my flame, perhaps this custody is how it should be."

Sara's wails turned to shrieks. Immediately, she pushed away from the window and shielded her eyes.

Both Spirits approached the frame this time. To the Future Spirit, what it saw was the same image that had frightened Sara: a foreboding graveyard shrouded in mist, but to the Spirit, its findings were unique. Though the image was that of the familiar cemetery as well, the Angel had returned, replacing her effigy and bursting with radiant bliss. As well, the field of gravestones was accompanied by other apparitions...many of them. Each stared in silence at the Spirit, while staying positioned at the spot where their mortal body rested.

"Do not fear," spoke the Future Spirit to Sara before turning to approach her and offer her some semblance of comfort.

The Spirit did not follow but, instead, left the shadow without the Phantom's guidance and soared through the window. It joined its brethren on the hallowed surface, weaving between the ghostly figures that stood like pegs in a board at their graves. Though the Spirit required no reintroductions, the inscriptions on their plaques were no longer iced over and now revealed their names. It recognized Henrich Gogel when reaching him before spotting Constance Tully, then finding Ebenezer Scrooge behind her, followed by Tommy Gaines, Priscilla Wong, Jean-Luc Renoit, and then countless others. The Spirit knew each soul, who gazed back with expressions that were nothing short of admiration and fondness before it noted the absence of a single chain link. Nothing weighed these spirits down, and there were no other signs of duress. Each looked to have ventured on in life as joyous and merciful mortals after having been visited.

Upon reaching the Angel, the Spirit confirmed, "They all atoned. Every one?"

"They did."

The beaming Spirit returned its gaze to the assemblage, but then was quick to observe that not every soul it had aided was present.

"Upon our meeting, you had mentioned that Sara's soul was of the future," reminded the Spirit. "Tell me, is that why I do not see her with the others? She has not yet perished?"

"Sara does live. From the moment your light extinguished, time upon this globe has halted while you seek your flame."

"Then she can still be saved?" The Spirit rejoiced.

"Do remember what I had spoken, Spirit... 'the purpose of your light was never meant for Sara but her brother.'"

Indeed, the Spirit did recall those words well, but it also considered that as long as Sara had a heart that beat and air to breathe, hope for her salvation lived on as well.

With enthusiastic vigor, the Spirit declared, "I no longer fear my past. Please return me to it."

"Do not disparage fear, Spirit. It is a powerful emotion; one that can weaken, but also give strength. Such strength will be required to resume the search for your light."

Upon her statement, the Angel's ribbons rollicked and curled. The Spirit readied for its continued adventure though it could not help but wonder, in more than rekindling its flame, what else might be learned. It would result in considerable regret should the Spirit never know whether Jonathan made amends with his family, or what significance there was in the one o'clock hour, or why he had been chosen to become the Ghost of Christmas Past.

"Will more than my flame be discovered going forth?" The Spirit asked.

"All will be made known. Do not despair."

81

"As well as the moment I perished?"

"Between life and death is where your flame awaits."

The Spirit reached for the Angel's hand. A luminescent ribbon ended its dance to fasten their bond. But before the radiance wisped them away, the Spirit recalled how the Angel had abandoned it at the marsh and was quick to ensure, "Will you be present with me?"

"Beloved Spirit, though you may not always see me, I never leave your side."

#

STAVE FOUR

The Flame

The immensity of the hall was first noticed upon their arrival, followed by its emptiness. The Spirit's gaze followed the gold moldings that trimmed an immaculate corridor to an elegant winding staircase. Oil portraits and landscapes covered the walls that reached to a third story. Carved into the wood railing that pivoted at six turning points were the intricate design of vines and leaflets. The Spirit returned its observance to the hall and the Oriental rug that stretched the entire length, woven to such an astounding measurement that it did not provide a single gap of bare floor; only around its trim could the Spirit see the stone tiles beneath.

It had been returned to the abbey, no doubt about that. Having yet to observe a single area beyond the ballroom, the Spirit surmised that Jonathan had once come from a family who possessed extraordinary wealth. Such abundance did remind the Spirit of a peculiar individual of considerable greed who had kept Christmas in a malevolent way.

A score of clamor from beyond the walls broke the peaceful atmosphere. Trotting horse hooves on gravel, rattling chain links, and spouting orders from a driver announced a carriage's arrival.

The Spirit's gaze followed the commotion through an open doorway at its side then peered beyond an intimate, yet lavishly dressed, dining table inside a cozy nook. Natural morning light doused the small room from a frosted window that filtered the sun's rays. The Spirit scarcely could distinguish the shadow of a

85

horse and buggy slowing to a stop as the driver had so demanded.

Merry gaiety soon followed from the high voices of a woman and a young boy, who cheered the new visitor. The fuss did not last beyond half past a minute before Morgan's distinct voice gave orders to "Take Jonathan's luggage to his room and have the cases unpacked while we breakfast."

By the Spirit's estimation, the man did not sound as over-joyed by the moment as the others.

"Yes, sir," replied the unseen servant.

The Spirit wished to clarify, "This is a different day than the Christmas I observed at the marsh."

"We are in the next year," explained the Angel. "All that you have left to bear will be of this time."

The Spirit found this news some of the most remarkable yet. "If I am to find my flame in the transition between life and death, then this will be my final Christmas. Do I die on this day? Is that how I become the spirit of all Christmases pasts?"

"All will be answered," reminded the Angel. "Observe."

What remained of the outside commotion entered the home and roared into a crescendo down the corridor. Coming closer, the family turned a nearby corner and came into view. Jonathan, still a child, though mimicking the Spirit's ageless appearance, had the entourage of brother and step-mother at his sides, while Morgan trailed a step behind.

"How were your travels?" Deidra asked. "Did you rest at all?"

"Very little," replied Jonathan, carrying inside a portion of his own baggage…at the base of his eyes.

The Ghost of Christmas Past

"We're so pleased that you made it in time for tonight's celebration. This Christmas Eves' Gala promises to be the grandest and most talked about yet."

"What have you learned?" Morgan Junior nosed. "Did you bring any books with you? I'd love to read something new. Daniel DeFoe has been my favorite. Have you read Robinson Crusoe yet? I've heard said that he has a new book coming that's wicked good."

"Morgan," protested the senior. "That word is not permitted in this home."

"Apologies, father."

"We had the staff prepare your favorite for this morning's meal. Haven't we, father?" Deidra injected, and then adjusted her gaze to include Morgan, who nudged a nod of agreement. "I do hope you are famished."

The family reached the Spirit and Angel's position then turned to enter the breakfast room.

White linen, gold china, silver utensils, and a glorious pink floral centerpiece decorated the round table. Once the family took their seats, a food attendant wheeled a cart through a second entrance, followed by a butler. An assortment of meats, cheeses, fruits, and pastries were served.

Dreary-eyed, Jonathan gazed ahead at the colorful arrangement.

"Wherever I had come from," spoke the Spirit. "Neither I, nor my father, look pleased by my return. Am I to discover where I've been?"

"Soon after the incident at the marsh, your father positioned you at a school that was beyond three days journey," responded the Angel.

"Had he learned of my treachery at the marsh?"

"No, but once his relief waned, Morgan became angered by the peril you had placed your brother in when abandoning him in the forest for your own amusement. No absolution would be given for allowing young Morgan to come within reach of his mortality."

The server wheeled the cart back into the next room, and the butler closed the door behind them. Once in private, Deidra boasted, "The flowers are beautiful, aren't they Jonathan?"

"Very much," he muttered beneath a weak smile.

"They are called Euphorbia pulcherrima. Word from the New World describes it as a Christmas flower. I think that's quite apropos. Don't you agree?"

Another weak smile of accord.

"Jonathan?" Young Morgan raised, ready to have his curiosity satisfied. "Have you been sporting? Do you cricket or fence? I've heard about a great game called bando. Do you know it? I would think it prominent in the university's province."

"Morgan," ordered his father. "Eat, please."

"It is," answered Jonathan. "But I prefer equestrian."

"No surprise there," snarled Morgan.

Deidra glared at her husband before addressing Jonathan again. "Are you not hungry? You haven't taken a single bite."

"Sorry. I am. Thank you. But I think myself more tired than anything. May I be excused to my room?"

"Of course," excited Deidra. "What a splendid idea. We

want you well rested for your first gala. I expect introductions with many young ladies will be quite possible, so we don't want you peaked."

"The boy is only thirteen, Deidra," protested Morgan. "No need to throw my son to the wolves upon his first pageant."

The expression of shock and revolt masked Deidra's, typically, beautiful face.

Morgan glanced at Jonathan's smirking face then gave a wink.

The Spirit bolstered with joy at the sight. "Why, did you see that? I'm not mistaken to have witnessed an interlude in our quarrel, am I? That is hope I just witnessed."

"Your interpretation is correct, but do not let that distract what remains of this vision."

"I wish to attend too," pleaded Morgan Junior.

"The hours are too late for you, but once you are old enough, you can," offered Morgan, but the boy was not comforted and pouted his bottom lip. "Do not disparage. You will be long asleep by the time guests arrive, and then, when you awake, it will be your birthday. That is cause for a much grander celebration, don't you think?"

Upon Morgan's words, Jonathan stood. He resumed his previous notion of retiring to his quarters by plodding out of the room, letting his frustration be known.

Deidra shot Morgan yet another look of discontent, the numbers of which he had lost count.

Morgan chose to ignore her annoyance and resume his meal, which the remaining two diners soon mimicked in silence.

"Is that all to this vision?" The Spirit questioned, befuddled.

"There is more."

The Angel stepped forward, and the Spirit followed. They walked through the wall and entered the ballroom left in disarray. Chairs, tables, and holiday flair had been placed into position and then left unattended for later arrangement.

Standing in front of the cold hearth, Jonathan retrieved Morgan's flute from the mantel then began to twirl it in his hands. A moment passed before the boy snuck the instrument into his vest pocket and strolled out of the room.

Once alone with the Angel, the Spirit offered no insight or comment, only silent introspect.

"You remain quiet, Spirit," she observed. "Do these memories continue to elude you?"

"No. I remember this moment now. Jonathan did not steal Morgan's flute with the intent to harm the possession as I first thought." The Spirit then became awed by its immediate realization, "There's a small box in my luggage, one that had taken me weeks to whittle from a block of wood. Its intent is to protect that instrument. My mortal self wanted the flute to be placed inside the box before presenting the gift to Morgan on the next day. I had wished for nothing more." The Spirit begged from the Angel, "When did I become filled with such devotion for my brother?"

"The incident at the marsh had opened your heart to regret. That coupled with the time spent apart from your brother had strengthened your bond."

"And the bond with my father?"

90

The Ghost of Christmas Past

"Shall be demonstrated forthwith."

#

The tables and chairs were no longer piled but arranged. Christmas flowers similar to the bouquet at breakfast were stationed on pedestals for display between each floor-to-ceiling window while bustling staff members materialized to make final preparations. Deidra and young Morgan appeared as well then stood near the fire-breathing mantel.

What might have appeared to be magic to some, the two immortals knew to be a rapid transition through time. The Spirit gazed at the clock that neared the three o'clock hour then peered out the windows to see the sun hovering just above the woods.

"Everyone leave us!" Morgan's voice boomed from the entrance.

As ordered, the staff exited through their nearest doorway, avoiding Morgan and the son he clasped firmly by the ear. With a strong twist, Morgan drove Jonathan forward. They reached the mantel then, like a marionette, Morgan guided his son's head towards the empty space where the pipe once displayed.

Deidra and young Morgan entered but stayed their positions near the door.

"What is the meaning of this?" Morgan demanded.

As Jonathan observed the shelf's void in silence, the Spirit recalled, "This was an impossible situation, I remember. Jonathan did not know whether to speak the truth, and ruin his brother's surprise, or tell a lie in hopes of protecting his own well-being."

"Out with it," ordered Morgan. "Do not waste your time in doctoring a lie. I have learned to distinguish your truths from untruths well."

Deidra made a motion to come to Jonathan's defense, but having witnessed her flinch out of the corner of his eye, Morgan played by her rules and expressed to her a look of disapproval. Deidra kept her thoughts her own.

"Has that school taught you nothing? Do you still think me a dolt to your crimes? What is it that you expected; the commotion of tonight's gala to hide your deceit?"

Jonathan gave no response during the interrogation, unintentionally fanning his father's inner fire.

Morgan twisted his boy around to meet his face. "Is the instrument still upon us, or am I too late in catching you in your deceit?"

Jonathan broke free and ran past his father too quickly to be recaptured.

Morgan's command chased him out the door, "Come back here, boy!" before the man followed.

Deidra held onto her frightened son with a mother's comfort as she begged, "Morgan, please!"

But her plea went ignored.

Time leaped forward again, but only by minutes to when Jonathan rode away on horseback. His ride carried him towards the forest with such speed that he was out of sight by the time Morgan mounted his own to chase after.

#

THE GHOST OF CHRISTMAS PAST

Twilight's domination over the forest had been in progress well before Jonathan slowed his stallion to stop within an arm's length from where the Angel and the Spirit waited. The boy's decision to halt had not been by choice but by necessity as the expression upon his face illustrated. His stare was hard and questioning, and went over and beyond the Spirit's position.

The Spirit turned to witness what matter had captured Jonathan's incredulous attention and became no less surprised to discover the sculpture of an Angel peeking through layers of trees, branches, and brush between them. The figure was the very same, the only Angel statue, it ever knew.

"That Christmas day, at the marsh, that was your memorial Jonathan and I observed within the mist's shadows," realized the Spirit when addressing the Angel. "It is real. That is why Jonathan could see your form. And yet, this marker, and the graven image from the netherworld, are one and the same."

"Indeed, Spirit," the Angel replied lovingly. "The hallowed ground from your journey's start was but a garden of souls you had touched across all time, in both this life and the next."

Upon analyzing the Angel's explanation, the Spirit felt as though its world had turned on its head. "Though I cannot remember, you imply that we had met before."

"Briefly," beamed the Angel.

"Who are you?" It asked, begging to be answered.

Her glow intensified along with her smile. "I must leave you now."

And before the Spirt could protest, or ask another inquiry,

or beseech her to stay, the Angel whisked towards her image and melded with the stone to assume its hardened state. But yet, not all of her glow had dissipated; a fragment remained behind her foundation, accompanied by the murmurs of a one-sided conversation.

Hearing the single voice, too, Jonathan dismounted then wrapped his mount's reins securely around the trunk of the nearest tree. He stepped closer but slowed his pace to a creep when the twigs and leaves crunched under his weight. Silencing his alarm, Jonathan entered a clearance, unobserved. The patch gave a home to many statues and headstones.

Once spotting Morgan knelt penitently at the Angel's base with a glowing lantern at his side, the Spirit accompanied Jonathan to a nearby tombstone where the boy crouched.

Distinctly, Jonathan and the Spirit heard Morgan pray, "Please direct me further. I know not what else to do. I implore your guidance, Elizabeth. Neither Jonathan nor I can continue in these conditions. I fear that, in time, there will be an event when our son will lose all sensibilities and pose a threat to those around him."

At no other moment had the Spirit and Jonathan been more alike than when mirroring awe-struck by the revelation. Then, as though able to read the Spirit's thoughts and to speak on its behalf, Jonathan challenged, "Why, father? Why would you keep me from my mother's memorial these many years?"

Morgan stood, startled, and then demanded coldly, "What are you doing here? Return home at once!"

The Spirit approached the statue with Jonathan at his

wing, who proceeded to ignore his father's stern demand, for each needed to see for themselves.

"Jonathan!" Morgan shouted, attempting to disrupt his son's path when stepping onto it, though his position could not shield the inscriptions large lettering, which bore the words:

ELIZABETH ANNE HENLEY-SHAW
Beloved Daughter Wife Mother
Entered Immortality February 9, 1707
Born October 11, 1689

"Why would you keep me from her?" Jonathan raged without demonstrating the slightest indication of honor.

Morgan's teeth clenched. "You will be dealt with at home."

"You will answer now," exploded the boy from a swelling of diseased anger.

"How dare you speak to me with such tone. I am your father!"

"And she was my mother! Why have you kept me from this place?"

Morgan remained silent; even hesitant.

"You fault me for her death."

"Absurd."

"Liar! You're nothing but a cruel man who is undeserving of any affection, especially hers."

Jonathan struck the ground. He then covered his left

cheek to shield against a second backhanded strike from his father. And though Morgan continued to attack, his weapon of choice became his words. "It was cruelty I wished to protect her from. Your mother was virtue; the most righteous woman I had ever known. She was as remarkable as an angel; who only carried love in her heart and never gave a thought of herself. She deserves to rest in peace and not be hounded by the likes of an irrational, invidious, mean-spirited child." Morgan paused, and frowned upon the sight of his son sprawled across Elizabeth's grave. "And now we have soiled her sanctuary, you and me."

Morgan sought support from the statue as he teetered off his axis. "Though I am astounded each day that Elizabeth could have borne the likes of one so selfish and insensitive, I find comfort in knowing that half of your being came from me and not her. I dare admit that you inherited the worst parts from myself."

"Is that why my given name was Jonathan? Might it not have been as difficult to accept me as your own if I did not carry your name?"

Morgan leaned over. He reached out his hand, but not as an offer to assist Jonathan from the ground, only to reclaim his lantern. He sauntered towards the edge of the clearing, demanding as he exited, "You're here now. Say your goodbye, then leave it."

Jonathan was not finished. Instead of doing as instructed, he climbed to his feet to shout a demand of his own. "Why was I, your first born, not given your name? Tell me!" Jonathan received no acknowledgement from his father. "Morgan!" He continued. "That should have been my name."

Morgan turned to address his adversarial son. "That was

not what your mother wanted. Prior to dying upon your birth, she requested that you be named for her father, the most influential man in her life. As much as I would have liked my first born son to carry my name, I loved her too much not to grant her final wish."

Jonathan's knees weakened as the heavy burden of shame pushed down upon him. He clutched onto the statue's base for support. "Why could you not tell me?"

"Had I known it would trouble you dreadfully," he paused briefly to consider his hypothetical, "I would have behaved no differently. That is how much Elizabeth means to me, and it should have been your responsibility to inquire about the roots of your name instead of assuming the worst." Morgan returned to Jonathan then laid the lantern at his son's feet, "You can use this to find your way out, but do not use it to find your way home. That dwelling no longer exists for you."

On that finality, Morgan marched out of the cemetery and disappeared within the murky forest.

The Spirit glided to Jonathan's side. Both stared at the space where Morgan vanished and shared atonement, but only the Spirit spoke, "I am sorry to have doubted you, father."

Jonathan lifted the lantern to his face. He and the Spirit stared at the flame inches between them. As Jonathan gawked at the warm glow inches from his cold nose, the Spirit gazed at the flame enviously. True, the little flicker of a thing did remind the Spirit of its great mission, but also, the Spirit admired the fire for its independence from fear, worry, hatred, love, compassion, dread, apathy. As though asleep in an upright position, the flame remained still and undisturbed from the world beyond its protected glass…that was until Jonathan opened the lantern door.

The Spirit watched the boy reach inside. His hand moved with hypnotic intrigue.

"How ironic," muttered the Spirit, "that you desire the flame as well."

A breeze entered and forced the tiny blaze to dance away from Jonathan's touch. The boy made another attempt when the breeze leaned the miniature scorch the opposite direction.

Frustration, the Spirit never saw coming, reached Jonathan as he wrapped his palm around the wick and snuffed the fire in a moment of maddened conviction. Jonathan then dropped the lantern and used his heel to shatter its glass.

To no avail did the Spirit try to remember what dark thoughts soiled Jonathan's mind at that moment. The delay between what the image showed and the Spirit's memory of that shadow had never been more trying.

Gratefully, the Spirit needed not wait long. Forced to follow Jonathan's return to his mount, the Spirit recalled quiet determination to be void of any emotion. Jonathan had focused his desire to be as free as the flame in the lantern.

#

The Angel never did return, and the Spirit found its presence stuck in a vision it thought long over. Hours had passed, beginning with a trek through the forest to the road, which had been prolonged when Jonathan lost his way without the benefits of a lantern to guide him. The Spirit had no choice but to join Jonathan in his travels. It kept at the boy's side like the most obedient dog, tethered by an invisible leash. Why the Spirit hadn't been whisked away and transported to the next inciting incident was the question for which it had no answer. For some mysterious reason, the Spirit was compelled to keep Jonathan's path as its own, all the way to the abbey, as Morgan had forbidden.

And yet, the Angel continued to keep her distance.

Had the Spirit not been a master of time, it might have considered that the elapse of hours slowed once Jonathan held their presence in the barn on the abbey's outskirts to observe the Christmas gala that thundered with merriment and music, as scheduled. Jonathan's thoughts turned to rot during those long hours, verified by the chilling fallacies he muttered.

"What lies you must have told to Deidra, father, which allowed these festivities to continue whilst I'm gone missing... unless I'm not missed at all. Perhaps you told the truth and Deidra decided to have enough of me as well. Perhaps that is a wish come true for all. But what is your wish, brother? I wonder if you desire the same? I think you might. If not now, then soon. And should my presence be vanquished from those walls then let there be no trace of my existence at all. Not a solitary article of clothing or possession that bares my image, or touched by my hand, shall be left behind. I will wait until the guests leave and the halls darken, and then all memory of me shall be erased."

And wait they did, but not for long. Whatever had ended the celebration prematurely was unbeknownst to any outside the abbey's walls, but end it did, which was as curious as it was abrupt.

Though no danger could be seen, the guests gathered in a chaotic cluster outside the front door to wait for their transportation to arrive and carry them off. All were on their way within minutes, leaving the abbey dark and vacated. Jonathan waited no longer than a handful of minutes before making his approach.

The grandfather clock tolled the midnight hour, and the day had turned to December twenty-fifth by the time the boy reached the large French windows of the abandoned ballroom to find one lock unhinged. The Spirit followed him inside.

It was an odd sight seeing the fire in the hearth left to expire on its own. On any normal night, the flames would be snuffed for safety's sake. But this night was not normal, far from it.

Jonathan paused to observe the remnants of a great ball, appearing every bit as grand as how he had perceived it from afar.

The boy did not wallow in envy long. Stealthily as a tiger, Jonathan prowled the halls and entered rooms to collect the possessions he promised to purge. The first had been his portrait from the study, no doubt, on the forefront of his mind. The hours required of him to stand perfectly still soon burned inside hearth in seconds. Linens, handkerchiefs, and emblems, all etched with his name, continued to keep the flames hot for the next batch of rubble.

For many reasons, Jonathan saved his quarters for last. Not only did his bedroom contain the vast majority of his personal belongings, but it also sat in proximity to the other family member's rooms. Leaving it for the end allowed more time for his parents to accept slumber's caress.

THE GHOST OF CHRISTMAS PAST

Though when the time came to collect from his room, the boy was not settled. When Jonathan approached the other bedroom doors, the Spirit had hoped it was with a desire to whisper a sentiment or a well wish, but the boy did not utter a single endearment. Instead, Jonathan pressed his ear against the doors, only to listen for stirring. Once satisfied by the night's silence, Jonathan gathered his remaining possessions and carried them to the ballroom.

Three-quarters past the hour, so clanged the clock's bell, as the Spirit stood by Jonathan's side to watch the large pile of effects burn. Coats, leggings, drawings, shoes, books, keepsakes; all of it had to go. Like a mirror's reflection, the twin images watched the flames peel away the layers, making their way to the center. The only items saved from a fiery demise were the clothes the boy wore on his person.

"Jonathan?!" Deidra cried in relief from the entrance. "Dear Jonathan, you've returned!" She raced to the static boy, wrapped her arms around him, and then proceeded to demonstrate her happiness by covering his face with gentle kisses. Gradually, the woman became aware of the items burning inside the hearth. Had she not, the Spirit might have guessed that Jonathan died by smothering affection.

"Oh, Jonathan," continued an empathetic Deidra. "We shall buy you new. I think it's just appalling what your father did, which he, too, now realizes. He's out there, Jonathan, right now, searching for you."

"He is?" The boy questioned, surprised.

"They all are."

"They?"

"Our guests! But not only our guests…everyone! The servants too." Deidra took a much needed moment. "Oh, this night. This dreadful, dreadful night. But, alas, here you are safe now. I am so relieved, and so will your father be. I only wish there were a way to summon him. He's been out in that cold for hours, ever since I made him go back before the party."

"But you saw fit to continue with your party," spat the boy.

"Only for appearances sake. It was with our greatest hope that you and he returned, but I could only detain our guest's suspicions for so long. Eventually, I had to tell the truth of it, and then they, our dear, dear friends, took it upon themselves to join the search. I only stayed behind should you return, as you did. Here you are!"

Jonathan did not share in Deidra's revelry but kept silent.

"Oh, Jonathan. Please do not judge your father harshly. There is no love like your first. Grant him forgiveness and show understanding in your grieving. You have that much in common for there is also no love like the bond between a mother and her son."

"Does such love for me remain?"

"Of course! Have I ever demonstrated less?" Deidra came in for a long hug. Jonathan accepted her grace and returned the sentiment that he would have liked never to end, but an uninvited breeze entered and assaulted Deidra's senses. "Oh, goodness me. Perhaps a bathing before bed? I will go outside and ready the wash basin while you retrieve a set of your father's night dressings upstairs. They will be considered yours until your others are replaced."

The Spirit smiled to watch Deidra plant one last loving kiss upon Jonathan's cheek before rushing out of the room. And though a delight it was to witness such gaiety lighten the dark mood, the Spirit radiated contentment when witnessing Jonathan smirk as well. All was not as the boy had thought. Morgan did not tell Deidra lies, but in fact, he had repented.

"The whole party," mumbled Jonathan, in stunned disbelief.

Yes, the whole party as well. All those present opted to join in the search. Never were there lies told or had devilish plans been made. Such diabolic inclinations were only true within the imagination of an insecure thirteen-year-old boy and, dare it to be said, a ghost as well. Yes, it was true. The Spirit did, for some time, share Jonathan's pernicious assessment of the situation, as though it had learned nothing. It hoped that offense would not affect it from finding its light.

"No!" Jonathan cried and reached into the fire. As the mound of possessions had been disintegrating, the fire revealed the hand-carved pipe case at its center.

Jonathan hadn't cared enough for the box to see himself burned--another could always be whittled--but the instrument... the pipe that briefly had a twin until burnt to ash inside the very same hearth, that piece was never meant to be destroyed. The boy had simply, and naively, forgotten to remove it from the case.

He had been quick, though not fast enough to exact his misdeed without injury. He let go of the box, but in its momentum, the container was hurled across the room. It tumbled to a resting position near the open window. Any relief that came with the hope of another wind gust extinguishing the flames was thwarted when, instead, the flurry helped the fire reach the draperies.

In the seconds it took for the flames to climb to the ceiling, Jonathan's awe-struck gawking inflated to panic. The Spirit watched no less alarmed.

"Fire!" The boy shouted but only ran from the room once frightened by the flames that billowed across the ceiling like a ripple on a water's surface.

The Spirit followed, and upon reaching the hall, Jonathan turned towards the staircase, continuing to sound his alarm for Deidra, or any servant who might be near. He scrambled up the steps instead of running out the front door; he was heading for young Morgan's room, a fact the Spirit did not need to remember to know to be true. If young Morgan had been put to bed prior to the Christmas gala, as both parents indicated would happen, then that is where Jonathan was going because that is where the Spirit would have gone had it possessed free will.

Polluted air greeted both upon reaching the third floor. Though brief, Jonathan did hesitate. How could he not when faced with black smoke that loomed between him and his brother's room at the end of the corridor? The sinister smog grew denser every second and tempered the lit chandeliers and wall sconces, for in the architect's grand design of this establishment did he place the ballroom fifteen feet below their position.

Upon reaching the last door, Jonathan threw it open with extensive force. Smoke and heat rolled out as the boy charged in. Between coughs, he called Morgan's name but received no reply. Once finding the bed, Jonathan pulled back the covers and discovered it empty.

"Morgan?" He stayed his position and called again, and then again, well aware of the many places a frightened and shocked boy could hide.

Jonathan heard his name shouted back. A reply… finally, but the cry did not come from the junior Morgan. Only the elder could shout Jonathan's name with such resonant authority.

Jonathan poked his head out of the room and into the hall that could no longer be distinguished as such. He made attempts to reply to his father, but the fumes interfered and choked the boy speechless; though, to his favor, the smoke did not have the power to dampen his coughs. Morgan's voice approached. The man was following Jonathan's coughs like a beacon. But as rapid as he was to reach his son, Morgan was too late.

The fire ruptured the walls, bringing with it a strong gust that took away as much smoke as it could carry. The burning rubble formed a barrier between father and son.

Morgan stepped as close as he could bear before reaching a hand and commanding, "Jump through!"

"I can't," replied Jonathan. "I must find Morgan."

"He came with me to look for you. He is safe outside."

The previous conversation with Deidra repeated in the Spirit's head, and when she had stated "everyone" joined the search, she had meant everyone.

The crackling echoes inside the hall were haunting. Jonathan glanced down at his feet surrounded by smoke and flames pushing through the wood floor.

"I'm coming to you," shouted Morgan.

"No!" Jonathan shouted with enough command to pause his father. The two each stared into the other's eyes: one with a look of warning, the other with an expression of understanding.

"The fire was an accident, father."

"I know, son."

When the floor gave way and Jonathan dropped below, the Spirit did as well; and during their descent, much happened. What the Spirit first noticed was the echoing toll of one o'clock. Somehow, the grandfather's mechanism had survived even when Jonathan did not. Another circumstance was the tether that bound the Spirit to its mortal self. The invisible shackle had shortened until the two entities merged as one, and it was then that the flume of flames surrounding them faded from angry orange to radiant white. Thereafter, and most curiously, came the awareness of being reborn when the Ghost of Christmas Past had its flame rekindled.

The Spirit stepped out of the fire and into the foyer of the abbey in time to see Morgan descend the staircase and race to safety outside. Waiting just beyond, stood Deidra and Morgan Jr at the center of a crowd watching painfully. A pull began to swell within the Spirit. It was being taken away from this world, but the Spirit resisted watching Morgan respond to Deidra's unheard question with a mournful shake of his head. Deidra collapsed in his arms.

Women wailed, men hung their heads low, but Morgan Junior did neither. Instead, the young lad peered at the Spirit, as though it could be seen looming in the fire, and waved good-bye. The Spirit gestured the same before vanishing.

#

The cemetery looked different. It appeared warm, and not so ominous as the Angel stood brilliantly at her place of rest, waiting for the Spirit's return.

As commanding as her presence was to notice, the Spirit could not help but take note of the inscription below her monument, no longer iced over.

ELIZABETH ANNE HENLEY-SHAW
Beloved Daughter Wife Mother
Entered Immortality February 9, 1707
Born October 11, 1689

"You have found your flame, Spirit. You no longer perceive Jonathan to be a monster."

"I see how I judged my life too harshly when leaving it. I understand what a mistake I made when abandoning my memories, thanks to your guidance and patience, mother, as well as the gift of Christmases past you bestowed onto me."

The Angel beamed as brightly as ever before.

The Spirit continued, "I know it was you who chose my immortal existence."

"As I said," prompted the Angel. "All will be known.

You are my son. I have always watched over you, Jonathan, and I always will."

"And who watches over you? You were once mortal too, mother. Who chose your position as Christmas Angel?

"Perhaps a story for another time. Your journey continues yet."

The Angel's ribbons danced through the air, fluttering past the Spirit, and then stopping near Sara's marker.

"And the brother you spoke of? The one who my light had been meant for? Daniel? What of him?"

"Perhaps with your flame's newfound knowledge, you will discover a way to service both well."

The idea boggled the Spirit. It implored, "Two in a single night? It cannot be done. It is impossible to repeat the one o'clock hour without disrupting time."

The Angel positioned herself on the monument's foundation without another word on the matter, no doubt, ready to return to her stately form. Immediately, the Spirit's quandary turned from disrupting time to a simpler fear. "Will we see each other again?"

"That is for the future, my son." And at the precise moment of her last word, the Angel statue returned.

The Spirit, though curious to see how it would continue in the real world, was more exhilarated by the prospect of leaving this existence for good.

#

STAVE FIVE

Restoration

W hat the Spirit had expected was as it had been. The third-floor dormitory inside the orphanage, pale and desolate, appeared no different than it did in the past, or the future for that matter. Even Sara made sure her position was accurate at the window's sill. Indeed, the situation was no less precarious than at any other time. The Spirit would calculate each move it made, henceforth, and every word it spoke. There was no allowance for error. Right down to the vibrancy of its flame's illumination, the Spirit would forecast what effects would come from its actions; thereby, keeping its light dim then restoring it to full brilliance gradually so as not to shock or blind the woman.

Sara turned once alerted to the radiance. Her red and glassy eyes saw what she did not want to believe. "What are you doing here? I thought I got rid of you."

Déjà vu. The Spirit recalled hearing those same words when Sara heaved them towards the image of its future, flameless self.

"I return to amend."

"Amend? You said I could extinguish you, but here you are. A lot of good this did," she spat before tossing the nightcap at its feet.

Though the Spirit did not expect to hear the clanking of chains this time, it was no less relieved by their absence.

Sara continued, "What's the point of putting out your fire if you're only gonna come back?"

111

"There is still time."

"Leave me alone. I don't want your help. It ain't gonna change nothing." Sara turned her back to the Spirit, and though she was ready to let go of her anger and this world, she made a point to be clear, "And don't catch me this time."

"You will be bound to this place forever," warned the Spirit, successfully stalling Sara's intentions. "Heavy chains will bind you to this room for eternity. I have seen this. If the choice is yours to pass beyond this world, you will never find the salvation you seek. It is not too late to rekindle what you have lost. This I speak of with certainty."

The Spirit reached out its hand.

Sara continued to stare at the cold surface below before twisting her glare at the surrounding ruins.

"Nothing you can show me is gonna change my mind," she warned.

"Not even Daniel?" Sara glared at the Spirit warily. "Take my hand and I will show you that not all is as it appears."

Sara made her choice, but the decision did not come easily.

#

Along with the Spirit, Sara dropped below the floor. The journey paused inside the foyer. The hall brimmed with the screams and laughs of festive children from an adjacent room. But the roaring antics of merriment were not what had captured Sara's attention. The hand-drawn decorations covering the walls were the same as from a previous vision.

"Didn't we come to this time already?"

In place of the Spirit's answer, the doorbell rang.

Miss Darnell turned the corner and marched for the door while yelling at any young child who crossed her path to, "Play elsewhere."

"Not this day," explained the Spirit. Though it was no wonder Sara could not differentiate this image from any previous when the never-changing sour disposition on Miss Darnell's face disgraced the scene.

It was young Daniel who had rung the bell. Miss Darnell appeared just as surprised as Sara by the boy's presence on the stoop, and he did not come alone.

Miss Darnell addressed a jovial young woman with sad eyes, who stood at Daniel's side. Her smile beamed as though compensating for a hidden sadness. However, no amount of contradiction could disguise her young age of thirty. In that, she was just as she appeared. "Mrs. Hicks? Daniel?"

"Merry Christmas, Miss Darnell," expressed Grace Hicks genuinely.

"What are you doing here?" Miss Darnell replied as coldly as Grace was warm.

"It's been a year. You said when we took Danny home that it would be alright if he visited with this sister after a year to acclimate. And it's Christmas day, even better."

"I brought Sara a present!" Daniel interrupted excitedly, showing off the gift covered in newspaper and scores of tape.

While Miss Darnell took a moment to glower at the poorly

wrapped present, Sara aimed her confusion towards the Spirit. "I don't get it. I never met Danny's mom. I never even knew what his parents looked like. This ain't my memory."

"My flame unveils images that connect to your past, as well as your memories."

Miss Darnell ignored the boy's excitement and proceeded to respond to Mrs. Hicks, "Indeed I did. Step inside." She made way for both to enter, and then Miss Darnell put on an act of bewilderment as she closed the door. "And Mr. Hicks? Where is he?"

"Oh, you know men and their sports this time of year," she explained apathetically, putting on quite the act of her own.

Miss Darnell donned a victor's grin when continuing to play along, "Of course. I understand."

"He's very excited to be a father. He really is," Grace defended. "It's just a tradition. Tom's a very traditional man. He's wonderful like that."

"There's no need to go on."

While Mrs. Darnell silently took Grace and Danny's thick coats, Sara recalled, "I remember this year, too. Some hot shot benefactor made a donation to the house this Christmas. We all got toys and a big dinner, and anyone older than five got to go skating at Rockefeller Plaza with the rich guy."

As Sara opened her mouth to mention more, the image interrupted.

"Can I give my present to Sara now?!" Daniel persisted.

"It's not much," explained Grace. "Just something small. I would...*we* would like to give more but allowing Danny and

Sara some time together is the better gift I think, don't you think so, too?"

By this time, it should come as no surprise that Miss Darnell stood as stiff as the wall at her back, though when no snide remark came from the house mistress, something was amiss. And right we were. After staring silently at Grace and Daniel for a brief moment, Miss Darnell squeaked with faux enthusiasm, "I'm afraid that is impossible, but only because of good news. I was never really one to believe in Christmas miracles, but just yesterday, Sara was claimed by a prosperous couple and taken to her new home."

"That's a lie!" Sara screamed.

"Adopted? Really?" Grace questioned.

Miss Darnell looked at the boy's face covered with disbelief. "Isn't that wonderful news, Daniel?"

"Why would she lie about that?" Sara screeched.

Daniel broke free from Grace then ran into the parlor. She hollered after him, "Danny!" But the boy did not stop. He called for his sister, and when no reply came, he called some more and continued shouting his search while Grace questioned, "What is Sara's new address? I'd like to contact her parents and see if..."

"That is impossible!" Miss Darnell interrupted. "The parents have requested a sealed adoption."

"Sealed!? Did they know she has a brother?"

"As you may remember, Mrs. Hicks, I explained that Sara was a troubled child, but as it turned out, I believe separating her from Daniel has taught Sara how to grow up and be responsible."

"Which makes her adoption even harder to believe when

115

people come here expecting to adopt a child, not an adult."

"Well, perhaps she would still be a child if you and your absent husband had taken the pair." Grace opened her mouth to rebuttal, but Miss Darnell quickly continued, "Regardless, I would be breaking the law by divulging such information, and I don't break laws."

"But they're brother and sister. There has to be an exception."

"No, there does not!" Darnell countered. "What you can't seem to understand is that if Sara's new parents were to complain, I could lose this house and all the children in my care would be sent away to who knows where. You wouldn't want that to happen, would you, Grace?"

Grace settled her offense. This battle was hers to lose. "Danny?" She called. "Let's go home."

But the boy did not come.

"Daniel!" Miss Darnell scorned.

Grace's lips stiffened. "I will handle my own son, thank you. He's no longer in your charge."

However, Daniel did listen and came, but then stopped at the bottom of the staircase.

"Merry Christmas," offered Miss Darnell. "Give my best to Mr. Hicks," and then left the foyer.

Grace knelt to Daniel's level and rubbed away his streaming tears. "I'm so sorry, but we have to go now."

"But Sara! You promised!"

When unable to find any words of comfort, Grace took her devastated son into her arms. Daniel did not hug back.

THE GHOST OF CHRISTMAS PAST

Awestruck by what she was seeing, Sara remained speechless as the house returned to its present and diseased state.

"Danny could never recover from this betrayal," clarified the Spirit.

"I didn't betray him! Danny knew I would never leave him without saying goodbye."

"Wouldn't you?"

Sara pivoted to the Spirit; her eyes enraged by the great offense.

The Spirit continued to explain, "In only the previous year did Danny reach out to you, but you could not deviate from the empathy you felt only for yourself and leave your window."

"I didn't choose a window over Danny," defended Sara.

"Not a window but the world you envisioned when staring out it."

Sara did not argue back; the point the Spirit made proved correct. However, she refused to shoulder all the blame, "What about Mrs. Darnell? Why did that wench lie to my brother about me being adopted?"

"Agatha Darnell believed she was protecting you. You had changed for the better without the crutch of your brother. Though misguided, her intentions were noble."

"Well, she was wrong!"

The Spirit held out its hand. The time had come to move on, and Sara had never been more eager to accept the offering, ready to discover what happened to Danny next.

They soared through the front door, and to Sara's enormous relief, left the place she despised more than any other.

#

The sun had long fallen. A single strand of colored lights illuminated the street outside the front window of a living room; the only decoration commemorating the occasion of Christmas, and not enough to bring joy to the gloomy and empty apartment where Sara and the Spirit stood.

"Who lives here?"

The front door opened before the Spirit could reply. It was thirteen-year-old Daniel who entered. He dribbled a basketball across the floor while making a beeline for the exposed kitchen. The Spirit's light helped to reveal the name "Sean" inked across its rubber surface once Daniel tucked the ball under his arm to rifle through the refrigerator.

"This is the same day I teased him at the basketball court, isn't it?" asked Sara, needing confirmation, which the Spirit gave with a nod. "I always thought his parents had some money."

"That assumption was made by you."

"Only because Miss Darnell told me that the Hicks didn't want to adopt me, not that they couldn't."

"The family suffered financially, even at the time of Daniel's adoption. They could not afford another, but Grace had desired a child more than anything and hoped a child would strengthen her marriage," which well explained Grace's undertones of sadness noticed in the earlier vision.

The phone rang. Daniel abandoned his quest for sustenance to gravitate to the receiver. His mood of apathy turned to one of resentment when reading the caller identification. He pushed a button on the phone's base. A loud beep followed to notify that the call had been transferred to voicemail. In the seconds it took Daniel to dribble across the room to a bedroom, slam its door shut behind him, and play music loud enough to rattle the walls, Tom Hick's slurred voice came over the speaker.

"It's me. You there? I tried you at, but they told me you were too busy to talk. Did you change your number again?" A brief pause. "Pick up if you're there."

"That's his father, ain't it? He sounds drunk," commented Sara. And true to her theory, bar chatter and the cracking of billiard balls could be heard in the background during the next pause.

"I said to pick up the phone. I need to talk to both of you; otherwise, I'll never tell you how sorry I am unless you pick up the damn phone!" Another pause, lasting long enough for a drink, as noted by the clinking sound of ice cubes coming through the speaker. "You know what? I don't know why I bother. All I wanted was to hear your voices. It's Christmas, and I thought maybe it would make a nice present, but I guess there're no gifts for Tommy this year. Merry Christmas."

The phone's beep announced the end of the message at the moment before the front door opened. Grace Hicks entered, and in spite of the booth collector uniform she wore, she could not be recognized immediately. The woman appeared to have aged three times the years spent. She set a single bag of groceries on the kitchen counter before removing her heavy coat (the very same from the previous shadow). Grace shouted, intending to be heard over the music, "Was that your father?"

She knocked on Daniel's bedroom door. "Turn down the

music please, and don't spend all night in there. That's no way to celebrate Christmas. Danny?" The music stopped, though he refused to respond further. "I'm going to make your favorite for dinner. That sounds nice, right?"

Still nothing.

"If you want to ignore me, go ahead. It'll be an hour before dinner's ready anyway."

The grocery bag tipped over, spilling a portable electronic device. Grace shoved the surprise back into the bag quickly then began removing the food items.

Tears rolled down Sara's cheeks as she watched. She attempted to wipe them away but could not keep up with their tide.

"You recognize her pain," the Spirit stated.

"He's a selfish brat!" Sara cried. "This is because Miss Darnell lied about my adoption, ain't it?"

"As stated, Daniel never could let go of the betrayal."

"What an idiot. Why couldn't he be grateful for having a mother who loves him?"

"You hoped he'd have been happier in life."

"No. I didn't hope. I believed."

The bedroom door opened, and Daniel stormed out.

"Where are you going?" Grace asked as he sped towards the front door.

"Out."

"Out where?"

"Back later."

"When later?"

But the moment for another reply was gone once Daniel closed the door behind him.

Alone, Grace did not deviate from her plan. She prepped Danny's favorite meal of meatloaf and mashed potatoes while Sara and the Spirit lingered. For some time, Sara did not notice that the shadow should have ended, not while mesmerized by Grace's struggle to prepare a merry feast while saddened.

"Are you trying to make me hate Danny? Is that the real reason why you're showing me his memories? Is it supposed to make me feel any better about myself?"

"That is not why we've come."

"Then I don't get it. Because that ain't the Danny I knew. My brother was never cruel like that. Please tell me this was just a temporary stage. Tell me he was just acting like any teenage boy and he snaps out of it when he gets older."

"I show this vision to you as a demonstration to provide insight," explained the Spirit.

"What insight?"

"You were not the individual meant to receive my light on this night. Your proximity to one another had confused my flame. My gift was to be for Daniel."

Not many words could have frozen Sara as stiffly as what she just heard. Try as she did to wrap her mind around the Spirit's concept, the weight of the admittance would not let go of their awe-struck.

"Losing you continues to haunt him. His devotion never wanes."

"Never? No matter who else suffered?"

Sara watched Grace, the innocent bystander in the universe's cruelty for her and her brother, open a box of dehydrated potatoes. She was ready to vanish far away from this image and reached out her hand.

In turn, the Spirit accepted. They strolled through the barrier that separated Danny's bedroom from the rest.

#

What had waited for them on the opposite side of the wall was Danny's room; however, unless Danny slept in a crib and used a changing station for a night stand, the space no longer belonged to him. But those hints were not the first to note a baby's quarters. Upon entering, high-pitched shrills magnified near Sara without so much as a warning. She cringed at the screeching melody and moved to cover her ears, but then resisted temptation, figuring the noise might be imperative to the scene.

Sara's speculation proved accurate once spinning to a rocking chair in the corner where an attractive, yet exhausted Clarissa Hicks coddled the hidden baby wrapped in a pink blanket.

"Is that Danny's daughter? Is he a father?" Sara asked, beaming with hope and eagerness.

"It is," the Spirit confirmed.

"And she's his wife?" The Spirit did not confirm a second time as Sara scrutinized the woman before announcing her approval. "Wow. He did good."

Clarissa reached over to a small side table that held her world at the moment: cleaning wipes, a cell phone, a glass of water, an ear thermometer, and a baby's bottle. She picked up the bottle.

"Let's try again. You've got to be hungry." She pushed the bottle's nipple up to the baby's mouth. Unfortunately, the crying persisted. "What's wrong, honey?" She set the bottle down and exchanged it for the ear thermometer. Within seconds the device beeped as the cell phone rang--both difficult to hear over the incessant screaming. The identification on display read: *Danny*.

Clarissa reached over and pushed a button then hollered to be heard, "She's got a fever, Danny. She needs to go to the hospital."

Danny's voice scratched over the speaker, "How high?"

"Ninety-eight point nine."

"That ain't so bad. You're overacting again, Claire. Remember, the doctor told us a hundred and one."

"I'm not overreacting. Just get home."

"I can't. They're making me work extra hours. That's why I'm calling."

Clarissa administered gentle bouncing to her daughter's care. "I need you, Danny. Come home."

"I told you I can't already. You know I gotta work. I have to go. Call mom."

Daniel ended the call. Clarissa looked ready to scream but resisted the urge. Instead, she rose to her feet, then paced the room while planting sweet kisses on her baby's forehead; one here, one there.

"Okay. So what?" chimed Sara. "So they argued a little.

This looks all normal to me. There's gotta be another reason why I'm seeing this."

And Sara had guessed correctly when the Spirit offered its hand. "Let us now to go Daniel."

They did not need to uproot. The nearly vacated dive bar came to them. No other installation exuded a false sense of comfort for those who had nowhere better place to be on Christmas. But one man, sitting at the bar with his back to Sara and the Spirit, did have somewhere better to be. He set his cell phone on the countertop next to an empty tumbler.

"Is that him? He's at a bar?!"

"I'll take another," ordered Daniel to Mike, the bartender, at the opposite end.

Mike paused to read the man like a poker player then disapproved, "Didn't I just overhear you say you were still on the clock, cabbie?"

"It's been a rough night. I just need a little Christmas cheer, from me, to me."

The bartender began to mix another Manhattan. "I get it. Holidays are rough."

"Some more than others."

"Wait a minute," spoke Sara, once catching a glimpse of Daniel's profile. She sauntered closer for a better look, then the shock of what she was seeing stole her breath. Sara knew this man.

"I don't believe it," she muttered before becoming engulfed by a rush of excitement. "It's him! He's the one who drove me to the bridge. He's the cabbie." Sara took a moment to reflect on the ride, struggling to remember what had occurred no more than an hour ago when she had paid so little attention at the time. However, one thing she could remember clearly…"He had a daughter. He named her Sara. He wouldn't stop talking about her."

Her tears returned, though this time, Sara was not so quick to wipe them away. She looked at the man again, just to be sure. "This is Daniel!" She shouted.

The bartender delivered the drink to the counter. Danny took a gulp. "What's he doing here, and why is he lying to his wife and daughter?"

"This is just one of many visits," explained the Spirit. "Daniel's greatest fear is suffering from the grief of losing another loved one. In time, he will learn not to care and push away all that he loves."

The joyful tears reached her lips, and by that news, they tasted sour with grief. "It's going to happen to him too, ain't it? He'll leave his family and become a drunk just like his father."

"That is for the future. I am the Ghost of Christmases Past," it reminded. "But I have yet to mention why I present Daniel's visions to you." Sara turned her attention away from Daniel to listen. "You were not meant to benefit from my light. Because of choices made in my past, I mistakenly followed from the cab the one who appeared to suffer the most."

"Yours was the face I saw on Danny's license," realized Sara. "So, I was never meant to live?"

"You were not."

Sara stepped back to catch her falling body; her legs,

finding it difficult to support her when under the heavy weight of truth.

The Spirit smiled. "You wish to keep yourself in this world now."

Sara returned her gaze to Danny then admitted, "More than anything. I don't want to die! I want to go back. I need to find Danny. Please take me back to the bridge, or wherever he is. I have to go back. I beg you, Spirit!"

The Spirit reached out its hand. Sara grabbed it and held on tight only to have the Spirit vanish when grasped and leave her stranded inside the bar.

"Spirit?" She begged, pivoting every direction in search of it, but the Ghost of Christmas Past was gone.

Mike entered through the back room's double doors, but he did not appear as Sara had remembered; he did not have long hair moments prior, it had been shorter and a smidge darker with less gray.

"Another," requested Danny, giving his empty tumbler a gentle push. From what Sara could tell by the back of his head, her brother appeared more disheveled then previously as well.

"Sorry, Danny. Bar's closing."

Danny glanced up at the clock over the bar that read the two o'clock hour. "For who? You're still open another two hours."

"For you. Go home."

"Come on, Mikey. Not tonight. It's been rough."

"It's always a rough night with you, so go home to your wife and kid while you still got'em."

"I mean it, Mike. I swear it's different this time. You ever watch someone kill themselves?"

Most definitely a strange question neither Sara nor Mike saw coming. For a moment, Sara considered that Danny might be speaking of her until she remembered that these visions were of the past, not the present.

Mike responded with a shrug.

"Well, I did, as of tonight."

"You call the cops?"

"No."

Mike's glare turned harsh and judgmental.

"I mean, I don't know. I didn't actually see it, but there were signs. And we were on the GW."

A chill raced down Sara's spine. Something wasn't right as none of what Sara was seeing made sense. She called again, only louder, "Spirit?"

Mike directed his attention towards her. "No more spirits. We're closing."

To say Sara was startled by the bartender's immediate attention would be a monumental understatement. And to rule out any misconception, Sara turned to see if someone lurked behind her. The room was, otherwise, vacant.

"What are you looking for? I told you we're closed," grumbled Mike, though Danny was not bothered while he kept to his thoughts.

"That's it?" Sara murmured as the Ghost of Christmas Past had done as she had asked and returned her to Danny. She was looking right at him; the very real and very present Danny.

"Show yourselves out. Both of you." And on his order, Mike picked up a crate. The bottles rattled as he carried them to the stockroom. "And don't forget to tip your bartender. Merry Christmas."

Once the cankerous man disappeared behind the doors, Sara stepped towards the bar.

Danny glanced over his shoulder, surely expecting to find a transient or drunk of some kind. To say Danny nearly fell out of his seat when seeing the woman he only knew as his "suicide passenger" would be a trite cliché, but that's how it happened, quite literally.

"You!" He shouted once obtaining his balance. "You're here! What are you doing here? I mean…I thought you…"

What had caused Sara to run towards Danny while a blubbering mess was as great of a mystery as the sum of her night. Sara has cried, yes, many times in fact, but never profoundly blubbered. However, the depths of which she cried did not truly matter. She could not contain herself, overcome with joy and happiness like nothing felt before. Any and all inhibitions were cast aside to revel in the moment she had only ever dreamed of.

In seconds, Sara had her befuddled brother wrapped in her arms.

Danny's confusion and overall discomfort came as no surprise. In some small way, Sara enjoyed watching him squirm, but once he started to make a dash for the exit, she panicked and shouted, "Wait!"

But Danny did not stop.

"You told me you had a daughter named Sara," she

128

continued, still in a state. "I know you named her after your sister."

Sara knew she had used the right words to stop him because through all the constant babble in the car, not once did he mention her...his sister.

Though Daniel did suspend his flight, he hovered cautiously at the door.

"Your full name is Daniel Raul Bello, and your parents died in a car accident when you were two, and you and your sister Sara were sent to live in an orphanage run by Miss Darnell, and you were adopted by the Hicks, but not Sara. They told you she had a family, but it wasn't true."

"Did you live there too? Is that why you're familiar?"

"No, stupid. It's me! We were lied to, Danny. Both of us, to keep us apart."

He said nothing. The torture of waiting for a response built as would the pressure of a busted gasket. Sara's tears returned.

At the moment Daniel permitted himself to believe the truth, he cried her name then resumed the embrace he surely regretted leaving.

The ruckus of crashing bottles roared from the back room. Misunderstanding the carryings on of the glorious reunion, Mike raced into the parlor, ready for anything. He stopped just outside the door and gaped at the tearful swaddle he didn't quite know how to interpret.

"Mikey!" Danny called once catching the bartender staring. "It's her! It's my sister, Sara! And she didn't do it. She's here! Standing right here. She didn't jump!"

"Yeah, okay. And we're still closed," reminded Mike

129

before returning to the storeroom.

"I thought you would leap for sure," he confessed. "But you didn't. And it's you! You're really here!" He stepped into another hug, which each sibling could not get enough of, but the next didn't last as long as the first when Danny burst with such exhilaration that it couldn't be contained. "We gotta...! We gotta...!" do something, but his mind raced, not allowing him to stand still long enough to figure out what.

Being the first of two, who realized the astonishment of this reunion, Sara had more time to gather her thoughts and suggested, "You need to go home."

"You're right! Claire! You've gotta meet my wife. You have to see her. She's beautiful. And Sara!"

"Yes?"

"No! My daughter, Sara! She's beautiful too. I can't wait for you to meet them both."

There was no more time to waste. Daniel raced out of the bar with his sister in tow.

#

The cab skidded to a spot outside the front of a rundown apartment complex. Double-parked, Daniel leaped from the driver's seat, then in a grand display of chivalry, opened the passenger door for Sara. Taking her hand, he did not let go when pulling her up a stoop like an eight-year-old anxious to show his assortment of toys, or perhaps his collection of things that crawled.

The locked glass door halted their excitement. Feverishly, Danny fished for his keys that were suddenly lost. He patted each pocket where they could hide, and not until it was the right moment for the laugh, did Sara pull the keys out from between their held hands. She jingled them tauntingly in front of his face.

Danny snatched them. "I can see you're gonna be a problem," he joked while wasting no more time in opening the property door.

A parade of inebriated chimpanzees would have been quieter than the pair who entered the very familiar apartment. From her bed, Clarissa sprang into the living room to find her husband with another woman. She whispered in a contained growl, "What's got into you? Everyone's asleep! Have you lost your mind?" Clarissa then focused her glare on Sara. "And who's this? What's going on, Daniel?"

He cupped her chin in his hands then leaned in for a kiss that, seemingly, was not returned in kind.

"Have you been drinking again?" Clarissa spat, pulling away. "You promised!"

"No! I haven't been drinking. I mean... I did have a drink, but I'm not drunk!" Danny chuckled. "And if it seems like I am, it's because I'm drunk with happiness."

Some point during Danny's ramble, Clarissa shot her eyes at Sara, who had stayed quiet until, "What my brother means to say is that..." Sara reached out her hand as an offering. "Hi Clarissa, I'm Sara, and I am so so happy to meet you."

As though he hadn't heard a word, Daniel put his arm around his sister then inhaled a deep breath, ready to announce to the world, "This is Sara! It's really her. My sister is here.

Standing with us right now."

Clarissa's chin dropped once her jaws unhinged, but not a word came out.

"It's really her," continued Danny. "She found me... well, I found her first, but then she found me, and here she is. Alive! And I wanted you two to meet. And this is Sara!"

"Sara?" A new voice spoke from behind. Sara turned towards the room she last knew to belong to the baby Sara, finding a fifty-year-old woman holding the hand of a sleepy five-year-old girl, who rubbed her eyes after being awakened.

"Mom!" Danny exclaimed when rushing to her side.

Sara anticipated the forthcoming introduction but did not require one. By the woman's kind eyes and caring disposition, Sara recognized Grace immediately, despite the fifteen years added to her appearance. However, Sara knew better than to make her awareness of Grace known for fear of coming across insane when asked how. Being thought of as 'crazy Aunt Sara' was not how she envisioned the start of this reunion and, therefore, falsified her first impression. However, Sara did not account for the unexplainable tears she shed once taken into Grace's embrace following Danny's introduction.

"I have asked for this moment for so long. I just knew my prayers would be answered one day."

Grace gave one last squeeze before releasing her submissive victim, as Danny leaned down and scooped his daughter into his arms. He smothered her with kisses over her cheeks, forehead, nose, mouth, eyes... anywhere he could. The little girl giggled hysterically at the tickling affection--loving every second--before

The Ghost of Christmas Past

Danny held his daughter up just high enough for the two Sara's to meet at eye level.

"Hey, snowflake, I've got the best Christmas surprise for you. Would you like me to introduce you to her?"

Apprehensive, Little Sara stared at the strange woman before glancing at her Grandma Grace, who eagerly nodded. The young girl then turned to her mother for final approval, but Clarissa was not so eager to grant her endorsement.

She stepped forward, and with deep scrutiny, analyzed every detail of this woman. And how could she not when homeless vagrants, escaped criminals, thieving con-artists were a common threat to her city? But let anyone who judged Clarissa for safeguarding her family gaze into a mirror, and then judge who it is they see jumping to Sara's defense when a wife and mother had only her family's best interests. After all, Sara did, seemingly, appear out of nowhere, and Danny was the type of good soul who would believe anything as long as it was what he wanted to hear.

All eyes were upon Clarissa as she continued to struggle with her decision, but there could be no mistaking the resemblances between the two. It was in their noses and eyes, as well as their pointed chins. Furthermore, Danny had believed this woman to be his long lost sister, Sara, wholeheartedly, and he was the only person in the room qualified to know. Based on those facts, Clarissa gave her daughter a nod of approval.

Young Sara then mimicked her mother's nod to her father, though with a touch more enthusiasm.

"Sara, this is my sister, and her name is Sara too." Danny then went on to explain. "You were named after her because, like

133

you, she is very important to me."

"Hello, Sara."

"Hi," squeaked the little girl, bashfully.

The euphoria of the moment caused Sara to beam in a way she would have never thought possible. So delirious she was with joy that Sara stated, "It's amazing how much you've grown," without consideration.

Her observation did not go unnoticed by the other three adults. Danny, Grace, and Clarissa shared bewildered looks; however, the moment was but a hiccup and long forgotten in their next breath.

"You're pretty," stated Young Sara, catching her aunt's breath unintentionally for Sara couldn't remember the last time she had received such a compliment.

"Okay," interrupted Clarissa. "Somebody needs to get back into bed and go to sleep so somebody else can come with presents."

Young Sara bounced in her father's arms with intense excitement at the suggestion of you-know-who, but as Clarissa reached to take her, Sara chimed, "Can I do it?"

Clarissa did take a moment to contemplate the request, but with the help of Young Sara's unarguable, "Pleeeease!" the request was granted.

The girl climbed into Sara's arms the instant she reached for her.

"Which way do I go?" Played Sara.

The little girl pointed the way.

The bedroom was appropriate for a little girl, and yet, not

so different from the baby's room it was less than an hour ago... to Sara. She laid her niece in the bed then pulled the covers up to her chin.

"Will you still be here in the morning?" Young Sara inquired.

Though she had not considered what would happen next, for the first time, Sara did not fear her future; and more than that, she answered, "I will," with the confidence of having told Young Sara the truth.

Young Sara smiled then rolled onto her side and closed her eyes.

Stepping away proved difficult. Greedily, Sara wanted to be in two places at once; here to watch her niece sleep through the night, as well as just beyond the door, to talk and reminisce and reacquaint the whole night long.

Two places at once, dwelled Sara silently as she thought about the persistent and wise Spirit who could perform such impossibilities.

"You know what, Spirit?" Sara whispered. "I don't think you were meant to help Danny. I think you were meant to help us all."

Sara reached the door then flipped the light switch. She paused a moment in the dark room, wondering if she might catch one last glimpse of the Spirit's remarkable flame. But when none came, and expectedly so, she closed the door to join her family for a night of enlightenment.

#

POSTLUDE

The Old Woman and the Spirit

D rawings in marker and crayon lined the dark hallway. When the nearby windows could project sunlight during the day, the colors of their creators' imaginative minds would greet any visitor with Yuletide cheer, but when night, the shadows concealed this litany of art, for no warm body should be about these halls. However, just on this singular occasion, an exception was granted.

A radiance appeared, but not more than a dim glow at first. The frosted-over double glass doors hampered the light, but as the illumination intensified, its warm brilliance burst inside and revealed the Ghost of Christmas Past.

It appeared with a sprig of holly in one hand and its nightcap tucked beneath its arm. The robes that burned with its harmless fire dragged across the floor when gliding through the hospital-like corridor. It stopped in front of a closed door that, surely, was not an obstacle for the Spirit, and did not delay its entry into the room for a second.

Prior to the Spirit's coming, the quarters had been just as dark as the hall; however, significantly noisier. The repetitious snores of some creature tucked beneath the layers of beddings rumbled the confined chambers.

The Spirit hovered at the end of the bed and gazed light-heartedly at the head of gray hair peeking from atop the sheets. On the nightstand just to the side, sat a digital alarm clock with red numbering on a large display. The minute turned from 12:59

to 1:00.

The hour had arrived, and the Spirit did not waste a second before intensifying its light to awake the sleeping being.

The Spirit was not greeted with the warmest of welcomes. Once reaching for her eyeglasses and resting them on the tip of her nose, the cranky old woman fixated her gaze on the Spirit, then demanded to know, "Who are you? What's going on?" She was not frightened at first, like most. This woman of eighty-three reserved her courage to further command, "Get out of my room!"

"I will not harm you," assured the Spirit tenderly.

"What do you want with me?"

"It is not I who seeks, but it is your misguidance, which has called me. I am all that was. I am the visions from days long forgotten, and the spirit of humanity from this season of joy. I am the Ghost of Christmas Past, Agatha Darnell, and I am to be your guide." The Ghost extended its hand. "Let us begin."

#

ALSO BY MICHAEL HEBLER

CHUPACABRA SERIES

NIGHT OF THE CHUPACABRA (BOOK I)
~ NATIONAL INDEPENDENCE EXCELLENCE AWARDS
WINNER, *2014*

CURSE OF THE CHUPACABRA (BOOK II)

LEGEND OF THE CHUPACABRA (BOOK III)

DAWN OF THE CHUPACABRA (BOOK IV)

HUNT FOR THE CHUPACABRA (MICRO STORY)

SHORT STORY E-BOOKS

RATTLESNAKE

WHAT ADAM WANTS

FOR THE CHILDREN

THE NIGHT AFTER CHRISTMAS (STORYBOOK)

Subscribe to the newsletter at
www.michaelhebler.com

As a tween, Michael used to "borrow" Stephen King books from his mother's bookshelf. Although he has not been clinically evaluated, Michael is positive that his adolescent self-introduction into adult horror had an impact on his dark sense of humor and love for things under the bed. Once reaching adulthood, Michael found an outlet in which to put his twisted thoughts to proper use, thanks to a college degree which proves that he had studied the importances of plot, characters, conflict, themes, and interactions.

But life wasn't always about the written page. Once Upon A Time in Hollywood, Michael had a career as an international film publicist, working on multiple titles for Walt Disney/Pixar, Lionsgate, Lakeshore Entertainment, Warner Bros., Summit Entertainment, as well as the 2013 Academy Award® Best Foreign Language film, "La grande bellezza" (The Great Beauty). Sounds exciting, right? Michael thinks so, too.

Michael also enjoys volunteering in his local community. Organizations he has supported include Meals on Wheels, Get On The Bus, as well as helping protect our animal population by aiding in the capture/spay/neuter/release feral program.

Coming Next

Return of the Chupacabra (Book V)